MEET JOHN DOUGH, SUPERHERO

A Political Fantasy

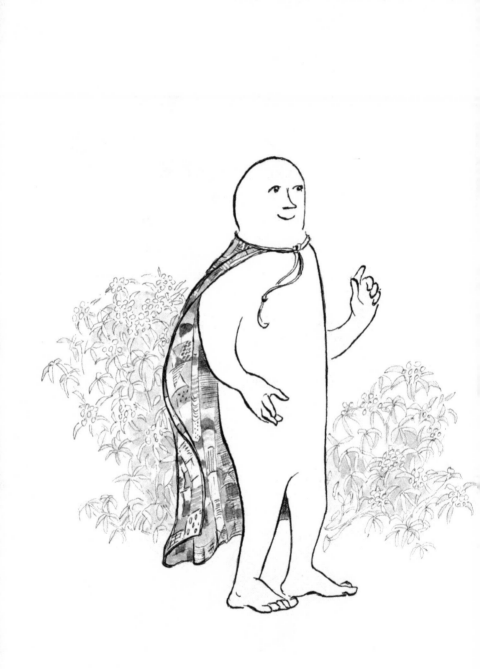

MEET JOHN DOUGH
SUPERHERO
A POLITICAL FANTASY

written and illustrated by
Lucy Bell W. Jarka-Sellers

NYOKA PRESS
PHILADELPHIA

Library of Congress Cataloging-in-Publication Data is Available.

Cover and interior design by www.DominiDragoone.com
Illustrations © Lucy Bell W. Jarka-Sellers

ISBN 978-0-692-97864-1

NYOKA PRESS
Philadelphia, PA
www.NyokaPress.com

Printed in the United States of America

10 9 8 7 6 5 4 3 2

For Mom

MATERCULAE MEAE VIRTUTIBUS MAGNAE

Do you have a dear mother, kind, devoted, and true....
—JIMMY CLIFF

In loving memory of Chris Allen, journalist.

CONTENTS

PART I

1. Airwaves 1

2. Augmentation 7

3. Rising 8

4. The Inner Light 10

5. Alive! 14

6. Rise Up! 16

7. Trees I 19

8. Trees II 24

9. Trees III 27

10. The Angel at Thirtieth Street 29

11. The Paxton Boys 31

PART II

12. Iowa 41

13. Neighbors 46

14. History Lesson 51

15. Fishing 56

16. The Fifth Kingdom 61

17. The Old Man of the Woods 66

18. Buddy and Larry 70

19. No More DIY 72

20. The Delegates 74

PART III

21. John Dough Goes to Washington 79
22. Heroism in the Rose Garden 86
23. The Oval Office 89
24. Second Thoughts 95
25. Aunt Alida..98
26. The Land of the Plant People....................100
27. Congress 107
28. The Press: Puzzles............................109
29. Wear It as Long as You Can 111
30. Baltimore 115
31. John Dough at the Capitol 120
32. Trumplandia Forever 122
33. Press Coverage................................128
34. The Mall....................................130
35. Rumor and Protest................................132
36. The Oven..................................136
37. Timely Assistance................................139
38. John Dough Speaks to the People 143
39. Entertainment................................149
40. Public Monuments................................156

Epilogue..160

Dear   Reader

They say that evil is a lack,
  mere lack.
Well, there's a lack, then, in
  D. Trump. Alack!
John Dough is here to take our
  country back!

They say that goodness is a fulness
  whole
That swells, expands, and makes
  its neighbors whole.
See John Dough rise, and raise
  our nation's soul.

Dear Reader, from my fancy
  don't depart.
Though clothed in fantasy, still
  Reason's part
Is major in my tale, and with it
  Heart.

If you will read my book from
  end to end,
I'm confident you'll find
  John Dough your friend.

LBW/S

2017

DEAR READER

They say that evil is a lack, mere lack.
Well, there's a lack then in D. Trump. Alack!
John Dough is here to take our country back.

They say that goodness is a fullness whole
That swells, expands, and makes its neighbors whole.
See John Dough rise and raise our nation's soul.

Dear reader, from my fancy don't depart.
Though clothed in fantasy, still Reason's part
Is major in my tale and, with it, Heart.

If you will read my book from end to end,
I'm confident you'll find John Dough your friend.

—L. B. W. J.-S.

MEET JOHN DOUGH, SUPERHERO

A Political Fantasy

PART

ONE

1. AIRWAVES

YEAST SPORES, THE KIND YOU USE FOR BAKING BREAD, CAN BE captured from the air just about anywhere. Alida trapped them in her kitchen in Philadelphia, Pennsylvania, by leaving out a mixture of flour and water in a bowl and covering it with a damp dishtowel.

This time, after two weeks of stirring and feeding (with more water and flour), she judged that it was ready to use. She put on an apron, turned on the radio, and started to mix her dough. The mixture immediately began to swell, suggesting to Alida that her yeast was unusually potent.

It was the year 2017 and the radio always spewed out the same kind of stuff. President Trump was threatening journalists, appointing his family members to important cabinet posts, and lying so consistently to the press and the people that no one even tried any more to pretend that he cared about telling the truth. Vladimir Putin of Russia had just assassinated another political opponent—this time by having him pushed out of an upper story window—and was funding a fascistic party in France (rightful home, Alida thought indignantly, of *Liberté, Egalité,* and *Fraternité*). Trump was gutting the EPA, easing restrictions on the free use of neurotoxins in food production and refusing to blame Russia for anything. There were new revelations about secret meetings between members of Trump's campaign and cabinet and Russian officials. Trump was settling a lawsuit for millions of dollars with someone or other that he had defrauded. There had been a spike in hate crimes.

The dough had already started to rise and bubble energetically. That was odd. Alida stirred it down with a wooden spoon and covered

it with a damp dishcloth. She left the radio on for the dog, who was comforted by the sound, and went upstairs to write a letter.

"Comforted!" Buddy said to himself, scratching the kitchen rug with his forepaws and turning around a few times before lying down. "I am a patriot. How could I be comforted by this stuff? I just like to know what's going on!"

An hour or so later, Alida was interrupted in her letter writing by fierce barking. She put down her pen and went downstairs. Buddy was crouched in a defensive position, paws forward, head down, barking menacingly at the bread bowl on the table.

"What's up, Buddy?" Alida said. Buddy growled; he wasn't going to move his eyes from the thing in that bowl.

"It's okay," she started to say, but then she saw that the dough had risen half a foot over the top of the bowl and was undulating. She approached the bowl cautiously and lifted off the dishtowel. She had always been brave. The dough shifted to one side of the bowl and then the other. Buddy stopped barking, figuring Alida had this one in hand, but contin-ued to watch, in case he was needed.

Instead it was the dough that was kneaded. It gave a little sigh as Alida folded it over and pushed it down. "This dough is amazingly strong and elastic," she said. "It almost feels as though it's squeezing my hands." Buddy stood up with his paws on the table, in order to see better, although this was usually frowned upon. The dough was still moving a little on its own, definitely quivering slightly at the far edge of the bowl. He sniffed. It smelled like bread dough.

"Today, in a tweet," the radio interjected into the pause, "the congressman from Iowa expressed admiration for European nationalists and their commitment to ethnic purity."

Alida was stunned. Even with all the terrible news, this was something new. A congressman from the *heartland* was openly praising a European *fascist* for being *racist*. It was *too* un-American. As though in answer to her unspoken question, the radio continued: "The Speaker of the House excused the tweet, suggesting that the congressman had not really meant what he seemed to be saying." Buddy growled.

Alida said aloud: "If not Congress, who can save us?"

At that moment, as though in response to her question, the dough stirred in its bowl and started to cry: a high-pitched, innocent, insistent crying—the cry of a little baby. Buddy paused confused, torn between suspicion and sympathy; Alida lifted the dishtowel that covered the bowl and looked in. On the surface of the dough

were two little eyes squeezed shut in unhappiness and a little round mouth open and bawling. Alida did what anyone would have done: she picked the dough up to comfort it. It immediately quieted in her arms. Buddy, no longer alarmed, looked on with interest. He had a soft spot for all baby animals. Alida saw that the dough wore some kind of token around its neck on a little gold chain. She examined it. It was oval with a little piece missing. On one side was "John Dough," on the other there was writing too tiny to read. She held the dough against her chest with one arm, so that its little head rested on her shoulder, and went to get the magnifying glass from its place by the dictionary. She read aloud:

FEEDING and RAISING DOUGH HERO

1 bathtub full of warm water
1 cup salt
1 lb sugar
10 lbs softened butter
10 dozens eggs
Flour enough to make a soft
 dough that won't stick to the
 sides of the tub

Fill bathtub with warm (not hot) water. Add sugar, salt, and yeast (Baby John). Add enough flour to make a thick soupy mixture. Beat in eggs and softened butter. Add as much additional flour as needed to make a soft dough. Cover with a damp cloth and leave for an hour or until dough is doubled in bulk. Punch the dough down and knead vigorously for 10-15 minutes. (You will not hurt JD, even if features are discernible.) Leave covered for two hours. Knead again.

A dough hero! Evidently a *bun* dough hero, Alida thought, noting the sugar, eggs, and butter. It was extraordinary, but these were extraordinary times. And hadn't she been longing for just this: that she herself might conjure some power to combat the dark forces that were gaining ground in America, emboldened by the grotesque but dangerous figure of Donald Trump? She laid the baby dough—now sound asleep—back down in the bowl and tucked him in with the dishtowel. Then she hurried off to buy the necessary ingredients.

2. AUGMENTATION

ON ALIDA'S THIRD FLOOR WAS A BIG OLD CLAW FOOT TUB. SHE filled it with warm water, added the sugar and salt, and then slipped in the dough baby who—she was relieved to see—gurgled happily as he began to dissolve. She carefully hung his token on the light above the sink.

Alida added the eggs and the butter and beat the whole mixture vigorously with the broom handle. She then added the rest of the flour, which she had lugged up in many trips. Buddy watched. This time the dough was too stiff to stir with the broom, so she climbed into the tub and mixed it with her bare feet as though she were crushing grapes. Buddy joined in.

When the dough became elastic and shrank from the sides of the tub, Alida got out and covered the dough with seven dampened bath towels. Then she tiptoed downstairs with the cozy feeling a parent has when there is a baby sleeping in the house. Buddy followed her.

3. RISING

AN HOUR LATER, WHEN ALIDA WENT UP AGAIN, THE BATH TOW-
els were tight over a bulge that rose several feet above the bathtub. She
slowly peeled back the towels and saw the visage of a pleasant plump
young man at one end of the tub, still rather indistinct. She drew in her
breath. He smiled at her with a weak but winning smile. Still wide-eyed,
she checked her recipe again to make sure that she was doing the right
thing: "Punch the dough down and knead vigorously for 10-15 minutes.
You will not hurt JD. . . . " When she was finished, she saw John's features gradually reemerge, even more distinctly than before. His body
seemed to have a little more shape too. "Thank you," he whispered
weakly. "Please start explaining what you need me for."

"I think it stimulates the gluten. . . ." Alida began breathlessly.

"No, I meant 'how I can be of assistance'."

"Oh, yes," said Alida. "Certainly." She had had a sort of instinct to
give her new guest privacy—perhaps because he was in the bathtub; but maybe she should be thinking of him as an invalid who
needed to be read to and otherwise entertained. She covered him
up carefully with towels and went downstairs to get herself a second cup of coffee. It was a daunting task, educating this bun dough
to save the country. She needed to gather her thoughts. When she
came into the kitchen, Buddy was lying on the rug with his head on
his paws and his eyes open.

"Today in Delaware," the radio was saying, "two Republican law-makers walked out of the state senate to protest the reading of a prayer from the *Quran*." Again, Alida was incredulous. One of the senators had afterwards complained that it had been "despicable" to invite representatives from a local mosque to read a prayer at the beginning of the session. "For heaven's sake!" exclaimed Alida, resorting to strong language in her shock and displeasure. More than anything else this sort of thing upset her—unabashed prejudice and intolerance under the guise of conservatism. "Who *are* they? They don't know anything about America!" She turned off the radio. "Come on, Buddy. Let's go upstairs."

4. THE INNER LIGHT

within the land of Penn
The sectary yielded to the citizen
And peaceful dwelt the many-creeded men.
—WHITTIER

WHAT DID AMERICA NEED A HERO FOR? THOUGHT ALIDA. THE president was attacking all the principles on which the United States was founded: freedom of religion, freedom of speech, a free press, the separation of powers—he was encouraging murderous despots around the world, many of whom seemed to be his business associates. And instead of checking him, as Alida had really believed it would, Congress was both shielding him and draping him with a cloak of legitimacy. And his followers had been bamboozled into thinking that there was something American about all this.

The country had started here in Philadelphia, and it was appropriate for a hero to rise here to save her: a Pennsylvanian hero. Alida addressed the bathtub covered with damp towels, trusting that the rising hero could hear her, and started from the beginning:

"The founder of this neighborhood where we now live arrived in Philadelphia in 1683. He was German and his name was Francis Daniel Pastorius. Pastorius knew seven languages and was interested in books and religion; when he arrived here in Pennsylvania he had a copy of the *Quran* with him. Pastorius came to join William Penn's

Quaker settlement. Unlike the Puritans in Massachusetts, the Quakers believed that God spoke to people in different ways. They also believed that each person had to follow the voice in his or her heart, his or her conscience. They called it the 'inner light'.

> *There's a light that is shining in the heart of a man*
> *It's the light that was shining when the world began.*
> *There's a light that is shining in the Turk and the Jew,*
> *And a light that is shining, friend, in me and in you.*
> *Walk in the light, wherever you may be.*
> *Walk in the light, wherever you may be."*

Alida sang the song her children had learned in Quaker Sunday school.

"So while the Puritans were burning people and books, William Penn was trying to make everyone welcome in his city of brotherly and sisterly love. The poet Whittier wrote a poem about Pastorius and early Philadelphia:

> *For there was freedom in that wakening time*
> *Of tender souls; to differ was not crime;*
> *The varying bells made up the perfect chime.*
>
> *On lips unlike was laid the altar's coal,*
> *The white, clear light, tradition-colored, stole*
> *Through the stained oriel of each human soul.*

"Make America Great Again!" Alida said bitterly. "Now they act as though it's an insult to read a prayer from the *Quran!*"

"There is a very beautiful picture of an elderly African American

Muslim at the Museum here. Painted by the revolutionary hero Charles Willson Peale. I will take you to see it. It's his most beautiful portrait.

"When they wrote their constitution in 1776, Pennsylvanians were adamant about freedom of religion," Alida went on, pausing to fetch a book from the next room. "'All men have a natural and indefeasible right to worship Almighty God according to the dictates of their own consciences ... no human authority can, in any case whatever, control or interfere with the rights of conscience, and no preference shall ever be given by law to any religious establishment or modes of worship', "she read.

Alida looked at the towels covering the bathtub, now rising over a nascent bulge, and hoped that John Dough had been listening. She had been thinking about these things so much since Trump had been elected and had tried to enact his Muslim ban. She had a lot more to say, but perhaps that was enough for now. She went downstairs on tiptoes, in case the dough hero had fallen asleep.

Buddy usually followed her downstairs, but this time he stayed where he was.

He had been listening to Alida with some impatience. There were so many really important things to explain to this dough man: health care, immigration, climate change, wars actual and possible. Francis Daniel Pastorius was just *not* on the list.

Buddy decided to start with climate change. In a way that was the most important issue of all: it threatened everyone—all the people on the earth, all the animals and plants—even yeast spores. He explained to the covered bathtub about Trump and Scott Pruitt and the Paris Accord. He argued rather forcefully for a sort of solution referred to as "carbon fee and dividend," and pointed out the reasons for its bipartisan appeal.

Alida took over when she came upstairs again. She told John Dough, who rose steadily above the top of the tub, about Pastorius's protest against slavery, written here in Germantown—the first formal protest against slavery penned in North America. She told him about the Continental Congress and the Constitution. She explained to him why the Continental Army had decided never to torture or mistreat prisoners of war.

Alida also told the dough about her father and mother—what good people they had been—and about her dear late husband. Occasionally—to Buddy's chagrin—she interposed a funny anecdote about her children when they were little.

Then it was time to knead the dough a final time.

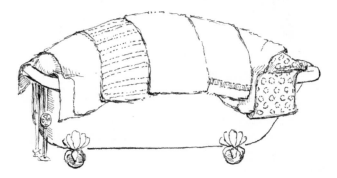

5. ALIVE!

ALIDA'S HANDS SHOOK AS SHE PULLED THE TOWELS BACK from the impressive mound of dough that rose high over the rim of the bathtub. Buddy stood by eager and keenly attentive. Had they hoped for too much from Alida's creation? A sweet yeasty smell filled their nostrils, and there was John Dough's smiling face: composed and benign, stretched flat over one end of the mound. Alida climbed carefully into the tub (20% of serious injuries to the elderly, she had recently read, occur in the bathroom). She held the rim of the tub with her hand to steady herself as she walked up and down on the yellow dough, now springy underfoot. Buddy took over when she rested. Together they pressed out the air bubbles and firmed up the dough. As they tromped and treaded and massaged, John's limbs and features became more and more distinct and firm. Finally, Alida and Buddy both climbed out of the tub for the last time and looked down at John. He lay firm and plump in the tub with his eyes closed. They could see that he had hands at the ends of his arms and five fingers at the ends of each hand. His feet were large and substantial with well-formed toes. His nose was gener- ous and the only part of him that was at all pointy. As they watched, his mass slowly stirred. All at once he stretched a great doughy stretch and opened his eyes. They were alert and lively. Alida and Buddy stepped back as he stood up and stretched again, lifting his arms way up in the air and extending his fingers. He smiled and softly sang a little song:

> *Walk in the light, whoever you may be!*
> *Walk in the light whoever you may be!*
> *With my soft doughy features and my yeasty yeasty jawn,**
> *I am walking in the glory of the light said John.*

Then for the first time John looked over at his creators. He climbed out of the tub and shook hands with each of them smiling warmly. Buddy was glad that he had learned, as a puppy, how to extend his paw.

---

* *Jawn* means, among other things, *stuff* in Philadelphia

6. RISE UP!

AND NOW COMMENCED, AT ALIDA'S MODEST HOUSE AT 413 W. Strawbridge St, those earnest conversations around the kitchen table that politicians love to dwell on at election time, in which hardworking Americans discuss important decisions that will affect them and their fellow Americans in the coming months and years. Or maybe the patriotic threesome was more like one of those secret societies of ardent idealists that springs up in totalitarian states. At any rate, this is the question they took up at Alida's house: What should John Dough do to save America? This was the to-do list they produced:

SAVE AMERICA

1. Remove Trump administration and egregious collaborators.

2. Health care, jobs, immigration, foreign policy, infrastructure, clean energy, environment, education: put sound policies in place.

3. Unify Americans behind essential American principles.

4. Bring the Iowan congressman to Germantown and convert him.

This last item was Alida's pet project. She couldn't believe that anyone could get to know her neighborhood without falling in love with it, and she didn't believe that anyone could fall in love with it without being moved to protect and venerate the beautiful American principles it instantiated—oh, imperfectly, of course, but still compellingly. And then, in addition, Alida had a recurring vision of the noxious Midwestern congressman dunked in some local body of water, the Schuylkill River or the Wissahickon Creek: sopping, muddy, contrite, realizing that he couldn't act like a—here Alida thought of some of the terms her grandson used for this sort of reprehensible character, none of which she could bring herself to use, despite their obvious appropriateness—realizing that he couldn't act like a *scoundrel* with impunity.

Number Two was, of course, Buddy's contribution, which he communicated through John. It was incredible to have an interpreter for the first time in his life.

While they talked, Alida sewed a cape for John, who had revealed to them that he could fly, thanks to the gaseous emissions of his yeast. Alida thought that a flying superhero should have a cape, and she decided to make it out of material that she had saved over the years for its sentimental value; for she had an instinct that an object as homey and loving as this method would produce must surely tend to augment the evident magic in John Dough's yeast. She put in a scrap from a dress she had made for her youngest daughter for the first day of kindergarten and scraps from her husband's plaid flannel pajamas. She put in a largish segment from a patchwork quilt, long ago too worn out to use, sewed for her by her mother when she went away to college.

When not in conference with his creators, John Dough read widely. Alida had supplied him with a stack of books, to which she continued to add, and Buddy had supplied him with an over-sized smart phone. Alida's daughter had given it to her, supposing (wrongly) that her mother would get the hang of it and enjoy it. Buddy, tragically, couldn't operate it with his paws, but he knew what drawer it had ended up in, and he brought it to John in his mouth.

At night John Dough slept in the bathtub under his new cape, which he moistened first.

7. TREES I

ALTHOUGH JOHN WAS A PRODIGIOUS STUDENT, AND A READER of superhuman speed, there was always one more book or article that Alida or Buddy considered essential. This couldn't go on any longer. The national news was as ominous as ever. It was time for him to gain some experience of the world. So, on a bright April morning, John left a note for his family and flew out of his bathroom window. Alida read the note with concern. There were so many things that could go wrong for a generous young dough man out by himself for the first time, even for a dough man of outstanding common sense.

Northwestern Philadelphia had the most lovely tall trees: beech, oak, maple, ash, tulip poplar, shag bark hickory, white pine. John flew low over them looking down into their branches from above. The deciduous trees weren't yet in leaf, just washed over with a faint pink wash. He flew north over the Philadelphia woods of Fairmount Park and continued until he reached the suburbs. Below him cars glittered in the morning sun on highways and in parking lots. The trees here weren't as large and there were fewer of them. He headed for a patch of green. It was a new development on a cul-de-sac. Just beyond the last lawn was a tiny patch of uncultivated scruff, in which a single tall pine tree rose above a tangle of sumac, brambles, and wild grape. John landed in the street and started to stroll toward the pine, passing tidy identical lawns and

asphalt driveways. Here too there was a pleasant neighborhood feeling on an April morning. Ahead a man ambled down his driveway in slippers to pick up the newspaper. A squirrel under an azalea bush paused in her digging to say good morning. As John got nearer to the pine tree, he made out a man with two children standing under it and looking up. The smaller child was crying. Something was lying at the man's feet: a tall ladder.

"It didn't work. He just climbed higher," he was saying. "We'll have to wait for him to find his way down."

"But what if he can't?"

"I don't think there's anything we can do now."

"Good morning," said John looking up into the tree too.

"Good morning," said the man.

"Our cat Pudding climbed up yesterday and hasn't been able to get down," explained the boy. His little sister, who was now in her father's arms, started to cry again.

"Maybe I could help," said John. "I'm quite a good climber." He had discovered that his flying tended to cause a stir, so he didn't expose people to it casually. Without waiting for a reply he gave a little spring and pulled himself up onto the first high branch. The family watched, impressed. John's consistency was an advantage as he climbed higher. He could squeeze between close branches just by changing shape, and scratches and pokes didn't hurt him at all. Quite high up he met a large fat orange cat.

"Hi," said John.

"Hello," replied the cat coldly.

John sat on a nearby branch in tactful silence for a while before saying as casually as possible "I could give you a lift down if that were a help."

"I came here to be alone," replied the cat stiffly.

"I could advise them to give you some space—tell them you'll come down when you're ready."

"That would be fine if I could get down!" said the cat.

"Hm," said John sympathetically and again sat in silence, looking the other way.

"Ignorant people shouldn't talk about politics!" the cat said suddenly. "I'm gonna go crazy."

John turned his sympathetic gaze toward the cat.

The cat, encouraged, continued: "The Dad—Fred down there—voted for Trump. Now he's disappointed, mainly because of the Russian stuff. His wife Sandy didn't vote—couldn't bring herself. We're all Republicans, of course. Sandy's all bent out of shape because of health care, but she has no understanding of the merits of the various bills. Fred, who understands less, defends everything Trump does—more so, you know, because he's starting to get the feeling that maybe he was had. He even went to a rally back in July. They argue all the time. I came up here when I couldn't stand it any longer. Then he came with the kids and the ladder and I went higher. Now I can't get down. I've missed two meals."

"How do you feel about Trump?" asked John.

"Oh, he's a disaster," said the cat. "Incompetent, corrupt, handing the GOP over to extremists, handing the midterm elections over to Democrats! Our foreign policy is a catastrophe. Honestly, I think the guy's nuts. By the way," he said, "my name's Larry."

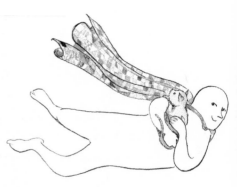

"John, John Dough," said John, and then added "Do you have someone to talk to about politics?"

"I wish! That might keep me sane," answered Larry.

"I have a friend whose passion is public policy. Would you want talk to a Democrat?"

"I would discuss politics with a *dog*, if he knew what he was talking about!" said Larry.

"We should arrange something."

"That would be amazing," said Larry. "Listen. I'm starving. If you're still up for a lift down...."

"Sure," said John. "No problem."

John held out his arm so that Larry could step onto it; then he maneuvered himself to the edge of the tree, bending over his passenger to protect him from sharp branches.

"I'm going to fly down," explained John.

"Well, that's something new," said Larry. "The GOP has to get the message about alternative energy."

John swooped up into the air with the cat in his arms. Then he flew in a wide curve around the tree with his cape streaming behind him and landed in front of the amazed family.

"Pudding!" said the girl holding out her arms to Larry, who looked back at John with an expression that combined embarrassment, resignation, and a desire for cat food.

"Just like Superman!" said her brother.

The man didn't say anything, but stood rubbing his forehead with a dazed expression on his face. John waved good bye and flew up into the air again.

8. TREES II

WELL, THAT WAS SUCCESSFUL! MAYBE HE COULD FIND SOMEone else who needed help. He continued east until he got to an older neighborhood, and it wasn't long before he heard another child crying, right below him on the sidewalk. This crying sounded sadder and more scared than the last, and he swooped right down. Two burly men dressed all in black, their bullet proof vests making them look even more burly, were getting ready to handcuff a man while two boys looked on with looks of devastation and fear on their faces. Everyone paused and looked at John as he landed right in their midst on the sidewalk. One of the burly men drew his gun. John stuck his arms in the air, just as he had seen on Youtube, but kept moving toward the men. There was a deafening shot, a scream from one of the boys. John was now embracing the burly men. The bullet had passed through his body, just cooking a scrap of interior dough and had stopped three inches into a good-sized sugar maple behind him. The men struggled in John's sticky embrace, clogging their guns and radios. Now what should he do with them? John thought of Larry. Of course, a tree!

The father ran to his children and embraced them. They clung to him.

"Stay there!" John said to them. "I'll be right back."

They watched John fly up beside the maple and edge his bulk

onto the highest substantial bough, some sixty feet above the ground. He then freed the men and placed them on the branch, carefully removing their guns, radios, and cell phones, which he hung on a higher branch. Then he flew back down to the group on the sidewalk.

"Don't be afraid," he said to the man, who continued to hold his sons close, one on each side. But the man wasn't afraid. If this was an angel, he thought, it was one you could talk to. He explained to John that the two men had been arresting him to deport him back to Honduras. He had lived here twenty years.

"I was taking the boys to the school. I haven't committed a crime."

"Is their mother here?" asked John.

"She's at work," the man replied. "Better not to go there."

"Where should I take you?" asked John.

"To the church," the man answered. "They'll help."

"I'm going to fly you there," said John.

"Okay," said the man.

John embraced the threesome, rose up into the air, and followed the man's directions to St. Francis Xavier, about half a mile away. In the distance, they heard the officers in the tree beginning to shout for help. They knocked on the side door of the church and an elderly man came out and ushered them into the basement, where they all sat down.

It was a sad scene. The man could stay there and a lawyer would come and try to help, but there was a good chance that he would have to leave his family and go back to Honduras in the end. The way he had been rescued would initially be a further difficulty for him, and it would be important to establish that he had never seen John Dough before and bore no responsibility for the intervention. John left his cell phone number for the lawyer and got ready to go.

There was nothing more he could do. The man thanked him warmly holding John's hand in both of his and crying. The boys cried. John walked out of the church and up into the sunlight. He flew back toward Philadelphia.

9. TREES III

NOW JOHN PASSED OVER ONE OF THE POOREST PARTS OF PHIL-
adelphia. The houses were old and colorful, brick and stone and
stucco, but many of them were disintegrating or boarded up. In
small back yards were broken appliances and sometimes tended
gardens with pretty old-fashioned roses, not yet in bloom. There
was a lot of trash everywhere, including little vials and plastic
baggies. John heard the sound of laughter and then a cry of fear.
They were sounds that shouldn't go together, and John went down
to investigate. On the edge of a small vacant lot was someone sitting on the ground propped against a piece of old car. Two figures
were standing over him. John landed just around the corner and
approached them on foot.

"Leave me alone!" The man on the ground said; he was an older
man. His words were slurred. He was drunk. He was also scared.
Two boys stood one on each side of him, teenagers. One was laughing, not a nice laugh. The first boy kicked the man then, kicked him
hard enough to make him cry out in pain. The boys had been intent
enough on their game that they hadn't noticed John walking up.

"Stop it!" John said and they turned. They looked at him with
eyes both hard and languid. The nearer one tilted back his head and
smiled slowly.

"Well! What have we here?"

John looked at both of them. His lack of fear was interesting to them and they paused, not sure what to do.

"He's an old man," said John. "Let him be."

The nearer boy got mad now. His face stiffened. "Fuck off!"

John reached out his arms then and pulled them to him. They cursed and struggled and then relaxed, the way fish do sometimes at the end of a line, before struggling again. John flew up into the air and looked for a tree. There was a black walnut at the far end of the lot. It wasn't a very big tree, but John saw that it was big enough. There was one upper branch that was strong enough for their weight, if he put them near the trunk, and high enough to make escape complicated—especially because of the branches below. They'd be able to get down eventually, but it would take them some time. They didn't struggle again. The flight had silenced them. John deposited them in the tree. He looked at them for a minute wanting to communicate, in case it somehow made a difference, that he hadn't acted out of malice, but he didn't know what to say.

The man on the ground, who had been watching this operation, recoiled slightly as John came back. He had a look of horror on his face.

"Why you all always gotta hang men in trees?" he asked and then passed out. John searched on Alida's phone for the nearest hospital and picked the man up in his arms. Once there, he deposited the man on a bench outside and informed the woman at the front desk. It didn't seem like much of a solution, but he didn't know what else to do.

10. THE ANGEL AT THE TRAIN STATION

JOHN STARTED TO FLY HOME, BUT HE FELT TOO SAD. MAYBE HE had done more harm than good that morning. He veered toward Thirtieth Street, where Alida had shown him the big train station. There he alighted behind a pillar on the east side and entered through one of the heavy brass doors. He walked to a bench facing the bronze angel and sat down. The angel was about forty feet high, with great graceful wings, wings really big enough to carry him. His head was bowed and he was holding a young man tenderly in his arms. The young man was hanging limp, his lips parted; he was dead. Below the young man's feet were flames, which surrounded the bottom of the angel's robe. The expression on the angel's face was sad, but calm: there was no protest or surprise in his sorrow. The angel's big hands gripped the young man's chest from both sides and you could see that the man was heavy from the way his flesh was pulled by the angel's gripping hands. Not too heavy for the angel to carry, though. John looked at the face of the beautiful young man and at the angel's face, which was very thin and sad and tender. The angel was going to take care of the young man somehow, but everything wasn't going to be okay. You knew that because the angel was sad.

John bowed his head and covered his face with his hands.

"IN THE OLDEN days," said a voice in front of him, when he had been sitting like that for some time, "I used to perch on his wings at night, but Amtrak has gotten stricter about that sort of thing."

John took his hands from his face and saw a pigeon looking up at him from the station floor. He had a fat dark gray body and pink legs and feet, and he was looking at John with his head slightly on one side.

"Hello," said John, wiping his nose with the edge of his cape and drying his eyes.

"Hello," said the pigeon. "My name's Ben."

"I'm John," said John.

"Nice to meet you," said Ben. "Let's go somewhere else," he added. "They'll start harassing me soon. They're very anti-pigeon here now."

"Okay," said John.

"It's such a beautiful day. How about we fly into the park together? I saw you flying in," the pigeon explained. "If you open the door for me, I can fly out and we can meet on the other side of the taxis."

"Okay," said John.

SOON THE TWO of them were flying together over the Skuylkill River, toward the Wissahickon Creek, creating, by this spectacle, a dangerous distraction for the motorists on Kelly Drive.

11. THE PAXTON BOYS

BEN LED THE WAY INTO THE WISSAHICKON WOODS OF FAIR-
mount Park, and John followed. They flew over the stream and then
veered right, following the climbing land up over rocky bluffs to a
high crest. There the pigeon landed on the substantial branch of a
tulip poplar tree and John sat down beside him. Below them spread
the wooded valley, around them the clear blue sky.

"Glorious!" exclaimed the pigeon.

"Yes," agreed John.

"This is one of the spots I come to," said the pigeon, "when I need
a pick-me-up. But tell me about you," he added, looking over kindly
at the dejected dough man. "Where are you from and what have you
been up to?"

BEN LISTENED TO the dough man's story.

"So, you're being asked to save America and you can see that it
won't be easy?" he said. "You're getting a glimpse of the weight of history? Your friend Alida only told you the good stuff? I could tell you
some stories. Human history is a sad story."

"The people who lived here—" Ben said, indicating with a gesture
of his wing the whole lovely valley below them, "the people who lived
here, before the woods became Penn's Woods, were the Leni Lenape
Indians. They're all gone now.

"Imagine the banks of the Delaware the way they were before the Europeans came: the massive tree trunks, the pure water, the Indian nations living their lives—Lenape, Shawnee, Susquehannock, Iroquois. The woods were full of birds and animals, and the rivers and streams were full of fish. Penn writes back to England of 'elk, as big as a small ox, deer ... beaver, raccoon, rabbits, squirrels ... bear ... turkey (forty and fifty pound weight) ... pheasants, heath-birds, pigeons, and partridges in abundance ... swan, goose, white and gray ... brands, ducks, teal, also the snipe and curlew ... sturgeon, herring, rock, shad, catshead, sheepshead, eel, smelt, perch, roach, and in inland rivers, trout ... salmon above the falls ... oysters, crabs, cockles, conchs, and muscles.' For fur and skins, 'wild cat, panther, otter, wolf, fox, fisher, minx, muskrat....'"

John realized with interest that this friendly pigeon was a scholar.

"And then the story unfolds as it did all across the continent—" Ben went on, "fraud and violence from the newcomers, reaction and terror tactics from the Indians, massive retaliation by the European settlers, eventually genocide. There are no more Leni Lenape here by the Delaware.

"Have you heard of the Paxton Boys?" he added.

John shook his head.

"That's how it ended here in Eastern Pennsylvania—with the Paxton Boys."

"Who were they?" asked John.

"A band of ruffians on the Pennsylvania frontier. Racist, even by the standards of the time. They saw themselves as doubly victimized: first by the Indians on whose land they squatted, and second by the elites in Philadelphia, who seemed to put the interests of the Indians' over theirs. A swaggering violence was their response to any opposition. They massacred one of the last communities of Indians in Eastern Pennsylvania."

Alida had told John about William Penn, how he had wanted to be fair to the Indians and how they had trusted and welcomed him, translated his name as *Onas* or *Miquon,* which means feather, for his feather pen. In the upstairs hall at Alida's house hung a framed sampler that she had made when she was ten. It said in careful cross-stitch, "Let us try then what love will do. —William Penn." John had liked everything he had heard about the founder of Pennsylvania.

Ben watched John for a minute, and then, as though reading his thoughts, continued: "William Penn *did* try to be fair to the Indians, protect them from fraud, pay a fair price for the land—according to an English understanding of the whole transaction. Any dispute between a European and an Indian was to be adjudicated by a jury comprised of six Europeans and six Indians. Penn had studied Law.

"And Penn admired the Delaware Indians," Ben added. "He learned their languages, which he thought were beautiful ('I know not a language spoken in Europe that hath words of more sweetness and greatness, in accent or emphasis, than theirs'), and respected their traditional forms of diplomacy, which he described with interest and appreciation in his letters home." Ben paused.

"But how could Penn not have seen how it would it end," he resumed, "when the Europeans cut down the huge trees beside the Delaware and built roads and towns and harbors in the Indians' hunting and fishing grounds? From the very beginning, Penn saw the forest as a harvest. And after Penn and the other gentlemen had claimed large tracts near the coast, why did he think that the waves of newcomers wouldn't want the remaining Indian lands? There were already European settlers here when Penn arrived and he knew how they could behave. 'The Christians here', Penn wrote, have already incurred the Indians' 'just censure' though we Christians profess to be concerned with 'things so far transcending.'

Among other things, the first Europeans had discovered the usefulness of plying the native inhabitants with rum.

"So, what happened?" asked John and, even though he already knew the end of the story, the middle was more awful than he had expected. Ben told him that, as soon as Penn was out of the way, his sons had cheated the Delaware Indians out of vast expanses of land. When the Indians saw what had been done and protested the injustice of it, they were deflected with obfuscating legalese and hypocritical moralizing. Angry and disillusioned, some had joined the French in the French and Indian war. Then the British army sent them blankets infected with small pox as "presents", instituted scalp bounties; even the scalp of an Indian child earned a reward. None of this was an exaggeration, Ben explained. You could see the tactics described in the graceful handwriting of the period.

"After Penn died there were still Quakers in Philadelphia who defended the interests of the Indians," Ben went on, "and the notion that they owned land, but eighty years after Penn came, there were only a few communities of Indians left in Eastern Pennsylvania. One of them was in Lancaster County. Already in Penn's time the Indians who lived by the Susquehanna River had been feeling squeezed by European settlers. It was in response to this that Penn had set aside 500 acres for their exclusive use: Conestoga Manor. At the time of the massacre this land was all that was left of the once extensive "Indiantown" by the river, and the population was down to twenty Indians.

"To the Paxton Boys the sight of Indians living on good farmland was an affront. The English and Germans might look down on their Northern Irish families for their manners and their unkempt homesteads, but surely they were superior to this vermin. They heard about terrifying attacks by Indians on frontier families and about how the government in Philadelphia failed to provide defense: the Quakers in the Assembly at Philadelphia had pacifist scruples or couldn't raise money for a militia because of squabbles with the Governor. And the Philadelphians, infuriatingly, made distinctions between different kinds of Indians, as though they weren't all savages, as though they weren't all in league with one another.

"The Indians at Conestoga Manor couldn't go out hunting for fear they would shot by skittish settlers. They wove baskets to sell to their neighbors and received welfare from the government in Philadelphia.

"The idea of welfare for Indians further infuriated the Paxton Boys, who were poor themselves. They were itching to clear Conestoga Manor for 'Christian' settlement. These Indians *were* Christians, in fact, but it turned out in the end that it was only white Christians that counted. Their ministers egged the Paxton Boys on in church: 'go and smite Amalek, and utterly destroy all that they have, and spare them not; but slay both man and woman, infant and suckling, ox and sheep, camel and ass.' They decided to take the Indian land in Lancaster by conquest.

"They arrived at dawn, fifty of them, and killed all the inhabitants they could find. Then they set fire to their houses. Among the charred remains of bodies and the burnt timbers was the treaty made between William Penn and the Conestoga, promising that the newcomers from Europe and the indigenous people would 'for ever hereafter be as one head & one heart, & live in true Friendship and Amity as one People,' and that the Indians would share 'the full & free privileges & Immunities of all the ... Laws as any other inhabitants.'

"But that's not quite the end. The Paxton Boys had only found six Indians at home that morning. Two weeks later they came back to finish the job. The survivors had been taken to the poorhouse in

Lancaster for their protection. The Paxton Boys broke in and killed them all: men, women, and children—and mutilated their bodies."

"And the people in Philadelphia? What did they do? What did they say?" asked John. "Did they care?"

"They cared very much—" said Ben, "the ones who did. And the Indians' neighbors were upset. In fact, when the Paxton Boys marched on Philadelphia—some 300 strong—to force the Philadelphians to cede to their demands, the pacifist Quakers finally took up arms—though bloodshed was avoided in the end.

"But the governor's attempt to bring the Paxton Boys to justice was half-hearted. And they never were punished. And the fact that they were never punished encouraged a wave of violence against the Indians that was the wave of the future. When the Pennsylvanian colonists turned their attention to independence and the fact that all men were created equal, they forgot all about Indian ownership of land. Then it was genocide in earnest. The Paxton Boys died in the Revolutionary War as 'patriots'—fighting Indians."

The pigeon and the dough man were quiet for a while then, sitting on the branch. Somewhere nearby a squirrel chattered angrily, and a wood thrush sang her flute-like song. A gentle southwest wind touched the trees.

"When I was a squab," Ben said after a while, "and first became aware of human cruelty and misery, I didn't talk for three days—horrorstruck. I think that's why I studied history when I was older. And history was worse: horror after horror. But it made it better, in the end, to know the truth, instead of sensing it lurking. And, if you understand the causes, then you see that you can't separate people into goodies and baddies. The Philadelphia Quakers were among the first to reject the institution of slavery; but before they rejected it, they got rich off it. We just have to keep trying to understand the forces that twist people toward cruelty, so that we can resist them—in ourselves too. You're a good dough man, John, and your heart's been stirred. Your friends raised you to be a hero. We need you. Don't be afraid!" He paused and then added, "'Walk cheerfully over the earth, recognizing that of God in every creature.' Have you heard that one? Alida will know it. It's a good one for you!"

"WELL, I GUESS I should be heading back now," said Ben, after he and John had talked for a long time more and the golden evening light had started to gild the branches of the trees.

John thought that, if he were a bird, he would prefer to stay here in Fairmount Park than to go back to the grime around 30th Street Station, not to mention the hostility toward pigeons.

"Why do you live downtown if you like the woods?" John asked. "Why don't you stay here?"

"It's a kind of discipline," Ben answered. "If all we animals went to live in the pretty places, city people wouldn't have any animals. Think what the city would be like without pigeons and sparrows and squirrels. In return, we sometimes find a pizza crust. Sure, pigeons live in the city for different reasons, but for some of us it's a spiritual discipline of compassion."

"That's interesting," said John. "I didn't know."

"But I can always come to the woods, when I want to," said Ben. "Sometimes I just need the natural beauty."

They sat in silence for a few minutes and then Ben began to sing:

We know the forests north and south,
We know the forests between:
Birches and beeches and maples and oaks
Blessed with immortal green.

Each spring the northland calls "Return!"
We heed the summons and fly,
Billions of birds in a towering flock
Hiding the sun and sky.

In May our nests are done, at last,
A lovely vision to see,
Hundreds of families perched on the boughs,
Massed in a single tree.

Our lives are lived to the pleasant roar
Of the sum of companionable notes,
Gurgling, murmuring, cooing, and calls
From thousands of brotherly throats.

Then comes the time that I love best,
The egg, the promising crack,
The featherless, skinny-boned, beautiful chick,
Soon with wings on his back.

The end of summer saddens all,
But then "return!" Is the cry.
And we rush toward the south of the warmth and the palms,
Blackening out the sky.

"That's beautiful," said John.

"The ancient *Song of the Passenger Pigeons*," Ben explained. "They're gone from the woods now too."

PART

TWO

12. IOWA

THE THREE PATRIOTS HAD DECIDED THAT THE IOWAN CON-
gressman would be their first project. Of all their plans, this one
seemed the simplest to implement. John Dough would fly over and
pick the congressman up and then fly him back to Philadelphia,
where Alida and Buddy, with the help of their neighbors, would work
together to convert him. They would start by appealing to the inner
light, but would move on to other kinds of therapy, if required.

It was the April recess and the congressman was back in Iowa.
There had been no getting around scheduling a town hall with his
constituents and he was dreading it. He had so far avoided these
ordeals on one pretext or another, but he had seen his colleagues
"town-mauled" on TV and it hadn't been a pretty sight. It would be
even worse now after the health care debacle and recent revelations about Russia. An aide came in to inform him that a large and
unruly crowd had assembled in the parking lot with signs and hats,
flags and noise-making devices. The room in which he had been
waiting had a view of the parking lot and when the congressman
peered surreptitiously through the Venetian blinds he saw what
seemed like fifty TV cameras trained on a group of constituents
who were posing with particularly well-made, witty, and insulting
placards. He could hear "DO YOUR JOB!" starting up; they seemed
to be rehearsing. A reporter from a national television station was

interviewing a farm family, who could have posed for Norman Rockwell. They looked aggrieved. He saw to his dismay that their youngest and cutest child had a little leg brace peeking out from the bottom of his overalls. They would be concerned about their health insurance.

"Goddamn free speech! Goddamn free press!" He said, turning away from the window. Then catching sight of the aide he coughed unconvincingly. "I don't feel too well."

"Sir, you have to go through with it."

The congressman knew that it was true.

THERE WERE TWO policemen stationed outside the Ada E. North Memorial High School, where the town hall was to take place. John Dough approached them on foot, having landed in a small municipal park nearby. They looked him up and down. He was clearly not from the district. Bob looked at Ed with an I-told-you-so look. Before the crowd had started to arrive, Bob had been maintaining to Ed that the auditorium would be packed with out-of-towners. He had gotten in something of an argument with Ed, whose family went way back in progressive Iowa politics. And then it had turned out, to Bob's chagrin, that not only were the attenders from the district, but, in addition, they all seemed to know his wife Joyce. She was the vice principal of the largest high school in the area, and although ordinarily he was proud of how many people she knew and how widely she was respected, he now wished that she was more of a homebody. The first constituent to arrive was a neatly attired middle-aged woman, somewhat heavy set, carrying a sign that said 'You work for us!' on one side and 'Not true' on the other, in the neat handwriting of a second-grade teacher, which in fact she was. Her face lit up when she saw Bob.

"Is that Bob Green?" she said. "Please tell Joyce what a wonderful presentation she gave the other night. It was just terrific!"

It had continued on like that, constituent after constituent. If Bob hadn't accompanied Joyce so often to work-related events, maybe they wouldn't have *all* recognized him, but she loved it when he was there to cheer her on in her professional capacity, and she was always so sweetly eager to introduce him to all her friends and acquaintances.

And then Ed, *the liberal*, hadn't ribbed him about it afterwards, as would have been natural. Instead he had dropped the whole subject, as though to spare Bob embarrassment, which was just condescending.

Because of all this, Bob was glad to see John Dough. John was golden-skinned and oddly dressed (insofar as he was dressed at all, Bob thought with pleased distaste). He was just the kind of person (if 'person' was the right word) who, Bob had been insisting to his colleague ahead of time, would be attending this event. Ed, on the other hand, was genuinely concerned, in his professional capacity, by the stranger's appearance.

"Good afternoon," said Ed. (When in doubt, make contact.)

"Hello," said John Dough, and he met each policeman's eyes in a natural friendly way. More than his open respectful expression, it was the subconscious effect on each officer of the sweet fresh smell of bun dough that was disarming. Bob seemed to be back in his grandmother's kitchen on Easter morning. For Ed the world just somehow became younger and more hopeful.

"Go right in, sir. The auditorium is straight ahead."

THE CONGRESSMAN'S STRATEGY was going to be to say as little as possible, so his constituents didn't have anything to run with. He would be calm and dignified, and the audience would look like a bunch of disreputable protesters.

Alas! If only the crowd really had been bussed in from other districts! Then Henry Loomis wouldn't have been sitting there in the front row looking smug. He had been that way since third grade. Henry had been one of the smart kids, and he used to taunt the future congressman for his academic struggles, calling him "ham head." When the budding congressman eventually got upset and punched his tormentor, it was he who got in trouble with the teacher. Now Henry was a successful lawyer and he always showed up for the congressman's town halls. Henry was sitting right in front of the microphone that had been set up for the constituents. He looked around the crowd with obvious enjoyment and then turned around to watch whoever it was who was being ushered up to the mike behind him. Suddenly Henry turned abruptly toward the front again and held up a placard that said, "You're still a HAM HEAD!" The congressman's face turned red. Anger surged through his body, "You asshole!" he murmured under his breath, forgetting that the little mike clipped to his tie would send his words booming through six carefully situated loud speakers. At that moment Henry ducked. The congressman was staring straight into the eyes of the little child with the leg brace and the overalls who had just been led to the mike by his mother. The crowd gasped in horror. They had heard about swamp-dwellers, but they had never imagined anything this heinous.

The congressman tottered. "God deliver me!' he whispered.

At that moment a huge yellow ball rolled at high speed across the stage, knocked him down, and scooped him up in its sweet stickiness. Before he could panic for lack of oxygen, he felt soft hands pulling his head out into the air. Whatever it was that had saved him was now dashing through the audience. Terrified constituents scattered, placards flew, screams and shouting filled the room. He was carried out the open door and almost immediately he and his savior were airborne. Below him he saw a crowd assembling; he heard distant sirens. For the first time, he questioned his assumption that he was in the embrace of a delivering angel. It was more likely to be a terrorist with felicitous timing. The land became small below him; he began to see the familiar patchwork quilt of American farmland extending for hundreds of miles.

13. NEIGHBORS

JOHN FLEW BACK TO PHILADELPHIA WITH THE CONGRESSMAN lodged in his dough: the lawmaker's head protruding from John's chest and one of his feet protruding from John's back. It was morning when they passed over the Schuykill River winding through the city below, and the congressman could make out racing rowboats fringed with white, where the sweeping oars dipped into the water. The banks of the river were bright green and the trees that lined it were still in tender red bud. Soon the Wissahickon Valley opened under them with its rugged bluffs and glittering stream. The woods, wearing the soft warm colors of early spring, extended as far as they could see. John thought about the Leni Lenape Indians who had lived here and how beautiful it must have been when the water smelled sweet and there were no highways. His yeast was native to this land and he couldn't help but respond to it. It was otherwise with the Midwestern congressman, who stared—eyes wide with terror—unmoved by the blandishments of Penn's woods. And there was more to alarm him as they approached Strawbridge St. He made out two rainbow flags flying from houses and got the distinct impression that whites were in the minority here. On one street he saw nothing but dark-skinned people. He wondered whether he would be killed soon.

John made a neat landing in Alida's small back yard, where Buddy and Alida, who had been on the lookout, were ready for him. Buddy raised his hackles and kept up a low growl as John pulled the congressman free of the enveloping dough. Alida, on the other hand, tried to put the newcomer at his ease by making warm welcoming remarks and telling him about the Quaker Service Camp that she had attended in Iowa as a girl. The congressman was too stunned to be much affected by their good cop/bad cop routine and stumbled along submissively as John guided him to the front porch. It was here, the three had planned, that the first phase of The Treatment would take place. The congressman was to sit on the porch swing with John on one side and Buddy on the other (in case he tried to make a run for it) and meet the neighbors. Alida had prepared fresh coffee, corn muffins, and bacon. She had figured that a corn product and a pork product would comfort the Iowan after what was bound to have been a disconcerting experience. For at least half an hour the congressman sat slumped and unresponsive. After a few minutes Alida stopped making lively conversation and covered him with a crocheted afghan, which he did not resist or notice. Suddenly he sat up and looked around. "Where the hell am I?"

"You're in Philadelphia, and we brought you here to meet some of my neighbors. We think you're going to like it."

"I demand to be let go!"

"John will give you a ride home, when you have gotten to know my neighborhood," Alida said firmly. The congressman looked over at John and shuddered.

"Okay, " he said.

"Now, just let me heat up these muffins and bacon for you and put on some fresh coffee."

When Alida was inside, she called her friend Mary and told her that it was almost time. Mary made the other necessary calls.

THE FAMILIAR SMELLS of coffee, bacon, and muffins soon overcame the congressman's resolution not to eat or drink while he was in captivity. He was just embarking on a second muffin—they were exceptionally good—a real old-fashioned muffin without too much sugar—the way his mother had made them—when a pleasant looking African American woman in her mid-seventies approached on the sidewalk. She was wearing brown corduroys and a bright green sweater.

"What do you see?" asked John.

" I see a dark-skinned person coming toward us."

"Hello, Mary!" called Alida.

"Good morning, Alida!" responded Mary.

"Would you like to come have a muffin and some coffee?"

"Sure!" said Mary and climbed the stairs to the porch.

"Mary, I'd like you to meet the congressman. Congressman, this is Mary."

"Nice to meet you," said Mary. "Hello, John." Mary seemed not to notice the congressman's lack of enthusiasm and adjusted a free chair so that she could talk to everyone comfortably.

"What a day!" said Mary.

"You can say that again!" Alida turned to the congressman: "Mary used to be a history teacher at the school where my children went. Retired now."

"What do you see now?" John asked the congressman in a low voice.

"An unemployed dark-skinned person," replied the congressman. John smiled at him encouragingly. This was going to take time.

ALL THE VISITS had been prearranged. Before Mary left, David Hill walked up the street. David was a trim white man in his sixties with tidy gray hair. He was wearing pressed chinos and a short sleeved plaid shirt. He had been an obvious choice for the conspirators. The congressman's mind was working fast: how could he signal to this man that he had been kidnapped?

"Hello, David!" called Alida. "Can you come by for a muffin?"

"Hello!" he called back. He stopped at the bottom of the porch stairs. "Hello, Mary! Hi, John." The congressman lost hope. "David" was obviously thick as thieves with these people. He seemed to be on strangely intimate terms with the black woman, even asking about her children.

Neighbors came and went. There were four more black people in addition to that Mary. They were all nice, actually—characteristically easy-going and jovial, the congressman reflected . . . well, except for the one who was kind of serious, and that other one who was, well, neither particularly serious nor particularly jovial. Then there was the Iranian doctor with the Jewish wife, and the woman he thought was a lesbian—because of the way she was dressed—until she mentioned her husband, and the attractive young blond who shocked him by mentioning her wife. There was even an Hispanic kid in a wheelchair who seemed to be friends with an oriental kid—*Asian*, they would say. It was worse than something on Public Television! The congressman was in a daze.

IN THE AFTERNOON, the dough man and Alida took him for a walk in a huge park, where there were all kinds of people out enjoying the sunshine. Black people out jogging. White people, Oriental people, Hispanic people. Black daddies with their families: that was surprising. The white people *did* look like liberals. Well, not all of them. In fact, quite a few of them looked like ordinary people. He saw a policeman from a distance, but the dog and the dough guy were sticking pretty close. Alida pointed out some fisherman on the bank fishing for stocked trout. (Even the fishermen were racially diverse!)

"I could take you fishing," she offered, "while you're here."

The congressman felt strangely relaxed. It had been a somewhat tense few months in Washington, despite the excitement of having an ally in the White House. And that town hall. . . . Honestly, he needed a vacation.

"I like fishing," he said.

FOR SECURITY REASONS, the congressman and John Dough were roommates. This unfortunately meant that the congressman had to sleep on the bathroom floor, but Alida had made it as inviting as possible, getting the least disreputable camping cot from the attic, and a camping mattress that seemed to still hold air. She had even put a little bouquet of violets on the windowsill in an empty spice jar. Just to be sure, Buddy slept outside the bathroom door.

The first night the congressman woke up at two in the morning, when his mattress lost its last bit of air. The dough man seemed to be asleep, so he stood up very gradually and edged stealthily toward the door. But, when he started to turn the doorknob, Buddy, who was on high alert, immediately let loose a blood curdling canine alarm. John Dough stood up yawning and placed one heavy soft hand on the congressman's shoulder.

"Why don't you have a seat?" he said kindly, indicating the toilet, "while I blow up this air mattress for you. It should hold until the morning."

14. HISTORY LESSON

AFTER BREAKFAST THE NEXT MORNING THE CONGRESSMAN smuggled a Sharpie up to his room and scrawled a Confederate flag—rather ineptly—on his pillowcase. John tried to draw him out about what the Confederate flag meant to him as an Iowan, since Iowa had opposed slavery and voted overwhelmingly for Lincoln, but the congressman just told him to go to hell. Although Buddy brought closure to the episode by holding down the defaced pillowcase with his paws and tearing it to shreds with his teeth, it confirmed their idea, based on a perusal of the congressman's public statements, that he was completely ignorant of American history, traditions, and founding principles. It was therefore arranged that John would guard the congressman on the front porch and Mary would come over and give him a history lesson.

Most of the neighbors had had enough of the congressman on their first visit. He was sullen and offensive and they all had excuses for not coming back. In addition, they explained quite sincerely, that it had been all they could do not to slug him the first time; they didn't think that they could restrain themselves any longer. Mary, however, was stalwart. She was older than the others, and, as she said to Alida, "I've seen a lot. I'm willing to see a little more, if it will do some good."

The whole thing with Stan and Jill had not been prearranged. Neither Stan nor Jill had met John or knew about the congressman.

They lived four blocks away and their kids had gone to the school where Mary taught. They just happened to be walking up the street now, with their black Lab on a leash: a friendly well-meaning couple of mixed European heritage in their fifties. Stan was a doctor and a runner; Jill had decided not to use her law degree when her kids were born and she spent her time painting large still lifes in oils, which she sometimes showed at the local cafe. Stan caught sight of Mary first.

"Heeey, Mary!" he said.

"Stan Miller, hello," said Mary. "Hello, Jill. How are you all?"

"Hi," said Jill. "We're good. Wait, this isn't your house, right?"

"I'm just here visiting my friend Alida," said Mary.

"Sure, we know Alida."

"She's inside finishing something up. These are her houseguests: John Dough and the Congressman," Mary indicated her companions.

"Nice to meet you," said Stan.

"Hello," said Jill.

The couple wasn't fazed by John, plump, yellow, and fragrant, in his patchwork cape. They were open to all kinds of people, and John was obviously a friendly guy. The congressman, unsmiling, his gray suit rumpled and stained, was more of a puzzle to them, but it was safe to assume—in this neighborhood—that he was also OK.

"It's a heck of a time to be in politics!" Stan said.

Jill raised her eyebrows slightly and nodded with a rueful smile. One of the few compensations of the current terrible political situation was the regular chance to agree passionately with her neighbors about something that really mattered.

Mary, with the unerring instinct of a master teacher in a tradition that valued classroom discussion, invited the two neighbors to come up on the porch and have a seat.

Their Labrador Einstein, who smelled Buddy all over the walk, trotted eagerly up the steps and stood expectantly. Buddy, on his part, sniffed Einstein through the mail slot and decided to stay inside. Einstein was one of those liberals who violently opposed the Republicans' new health care plan, but couldn't describe a single feature of it. Not only that, but Einstein's good-natured brown eyes would glaze over if Buddy tried to explain it. It was frustrating—especially now—to talk to dogs like that. Buddy felt that they undermined the cause.

"It makes me sick!" Jill was saying. "You know where we should build a wall? We should just build a wall around the middle of the country—around all those—I know it sounds bad—but around all those *stupid* people who voted for Trump!"

The congressman felt angry now, but more relieved than angry. He felt on solid ground for the first time since he had driven over to the North High School—it seemed like years ago. Here undeniably was a liberal coastal elite, showing scorn—unfeeling scorn—for his constituency. And what the hell was her husband wearing on his feet? His green sneakers had separate little compartments for each toe. It made him look like a lizard. The congressman smiled. He just hated these people! Now things were looking up. The black lady was beginning to say something. He listened.

"Of course, Pennsylvania went for Trump," Mary pointed out.

"Not Philadelphia!" said Jill.

"But still—I mean, if we were building a wall, would it separate Chestnut Hill from Wyndmoor?"

"Well, no one wants a wall, of course," Stan said. Jill nodded. "We need to reach out to the Trump voters," he continued. "The election showed us that. We need to show them that we're not prejudiced and condescending elites, who aren't willing to take the time to understand the challenges they face."

"You need to show them that pigs don't have snouts!" thought the congressman with satisfaction.

"There are many causes," Stan went on, "for the ignorance and prejudice that characterize Middle America. Simple boredom may account for much of the red neck agenda. There's just not a lot to do out there. They say that boredom's the primary cause of the opioid crisis. And then their brand of Christianity leads to a sort of us-versus-them mentality."

"It is a big area we're talking about, with varying traditions," Mary pointed out. "Take Iowa."

"Yes, take Iowa!" Jill said, shaking her head sadly.

"Iowa has a long progressive tradition," Mary continued. "They were the second state in the nation to repeal legislation against interracial marriage—way ahead of other states. The first woman elected to public office was an Iowan. More recently, they were one of the first three states to recognize gay marriage by court order. And these really are just examples. The list goes on and on. Did you know that the first mosque in the US was in Iowa?"

The congressman had mixed feelings. He was glad to see his state defended, but these weren't the grounds he would have put forward.

"I had no idea," said Jill with sincere interest.

"That's why it's good to talk to a history teacher," said Stan.

"Yeah, Iowa's okay," said the congressman suddenly and aggressively from the porch swing, "as long as we can keep up the birth rate, protect our culture, and ICE the spics."

Stan looked at him for a minute and then shook his head. He admired that kind of biting irony. He was too mild-mannered to pull it off himself.

"Ha ha! You nailed it," he said. "But you know, I guess Mary's telling us that there's another tradition out there too, one more in keeping with our national values."

"Our national values?" asked the congressman with disgust.

"I know the founding fathers had problems," Stan said apologetically, trying to reassure this sardonic radical, "but still they were on the right track when they talked about the dignity and equality of all people. I guess we can still value their insights even if they failed to live up to them."

"WHAT STUPID JERKS!" EXCLAIMED THE CONGRESSMEN WHEN the visitors left.

"It's true that they were saying some ignorant things," said Mary, "and I don't blame you for being offended, but they're well-meaning people, and they're willing to learn. That's a lot, isn't it, being willing to learn?"

John Dough looked at Mary with admiration and affection. Some people were so smart and so persistent.

The congressman was struck by Mary too. She was the first teacher he had ever had who hadn't treated him like a bad boy, even when he had done his best to earn that designation.

As for Mary, she knew she hadn't covered the material she had intended to in the lesson, but real engagement on the part of the students in discussion about questions that mattered was the most important thing in the long run, as she had learned from many years of experience.

15. FISHING

THEY HAD ALWAYS HAD THE IDEA THAT THE CONGRESSMAN'S conversion would be effected in three steps:

1. Meet the neighbors
2. History Lesson
3. Culminating transformative experience

But they had never come up with a good plan for Step 3, and now it was hard to confer with each other about the question, because they couldn't leave their prisoner alone.

"Maybe I should just take him fishing," Alida whispered, when the congressman was in the bathroom.

"What were you thinking?" whispered John back.

"I don't know," said Alida. "It can mean a lot to a person to catch a fish."

Buddy was skeptical. Alida had so much faith in the power of little things to spark the inner light.

"Google *deprogramming*," he whispered to John later, "or maybe *deprogramming psychological study*."

John didn't find anything helpful, though—just some disturbing stories about cults.

So, the next day, Alida collected her fishing gear and they all went down to the Wissahickon Creek together under a gray and menacing sky. Alida really had made a lasting impression on several acquaintances by taking them fishing, but they had all been under ten years old and none of them had had even a passing interest in white supremacy.

There were quite a few people down at the creek despite the threatening weather. Fishermen are as intrepid as joggers and dog walkers. The congressmen looked over at the older African American man and his younger companion who were fishing downstream and said in a marked way,

"And here we have *all Philadelphia!*"

Alida looked at him sharply. She didn't like the way he had said that. The congressman registered her look. It had been frustratingly difficult, in general, to get a reaction out of Alida, and the congressman, like most bullies, thrived on provocation and reaction.

John sat down on the bank and gazed contentedly on the moving water and the overhanging trees, while Buddy and Alida and the congressman made their way out onto a flat rock that jutted out into a deep pool. This was a promising spot for fish, thought Alida, who, in her generous way, really wanted the congressman to be successful. She picked out a handsome fly from her fly box and began to tie it onto the leader.

The congressman, meanwhile, was trying to think of a good way to make Alida mad. He wasn't feeling very inspired. He had had success in Washington praising the European right for xenophobia, but this liberal old lady probably didn't know enough about politics to be offended by comments on international affairs. The n-word worked every time, but it had become such a cliché. Oh, what the hell! He didn't have to be brilliant all the time! He felt the sensations he always felt when he was moved to bear witness against common decency: a little flutter in his stomach and a quiver in his hands.

"Alida," he said, looking at her more directly than he usually did, "your friend Mary is pretty smart for a n—...."

Alida didn't let him finish the word. She shoved him quickly with her shoulder, instinctively protecting the fishing rod in her hands. The congressman, though taken by surprise, would have recovered his balance, had Buddy not followed up with a quick thrust of the forepaws on the congressman's chest, knocking him backward into the brown pool.

When the congressman's face emerged from the water again it was wild with rage. The younger of the two fishermen ran over.

"Need a hand?"

"Get the hell away from me!" the congressman roared, treading water and gulping.

"We'll have to," replied the man. "You've messed up the fishing."

The water wasn't deep, and the congressman soon found his footing. Buddy braced himself, in case he would have to come to the defense of his mistress. But the congressman wasn't going to fight with an old lady. He spied John on the bank and made his way toward him, his head lowered like an angry bull's, his wet trousers clinging to his legs, his shoes squishy. As soon as he was on dry land, he flew at John.

"You!" he exclaimed with concentrated hatred. And he punched John again and again with all his might.

It feels good to dough to be punched, of course, but John didn't let on. He fought back just enough to give his adversary scope and satisfaction in the struggle like a kindly daddy wrestling with his toddler before bed. To the congressman, though, it felt like life and death. He gripped the dough man's arms with all his strength and pulled and wrenched and twisted. He kicked his legs. He butted him with his angry head.

A graceful bridge of local gray stone, built by the Works Progress Administration under FDR, spanned the creek above the pool. It was here that a crowd of park-goers had congregated to watch the spectacle. Alida and Buddy soon joined them. No one had phone service here, but they wouldn't have called the police anyway. The crowd could tell that there was something special about this fight: a psychological drama of rare intensity was unfolding before them. They watched enthralled.

Was the dough man really changing shape in his hands? Or was it just a trick of the congressman's strained imagination? In any case, the congressman's adversary seemed to take on, in succession, all the demons that haunted his unhappy psyche.

"I am not! I am not!" he cried, flailing at the dough man with his fists. "I am not a ham head!" Then the congressman turned in fury on "Mr. Burroughs." He seemed to be a math teacher, judging from the congressman's disjointed exclamations. John Dough continued to enable the maximum expenditure of energy on his assailant's part, deftly giving way and standing firm in turn, now throwing a soft punch, now receiving a hard one.

"You stuck up Ivy League son of a bitch!" the congressman yelled, grabbing John Dough's arms and kicking his legs. John guessed that they had moved on to the congressman's Washington foes now.

Once he simply cried out, "Dad!"

A steady rain began to fall. This was not enough to dislodge the fascinated crowd on the bridge. Their numbers continued to grow. All of a sudden, they saw the man in the wet clothes lurch back from his adversary. He paused, exhausted, gasping, his eyes wide. Rain streamed down his face. The big yellow man in the cape stood still for a moment and then took a step forward. Slowly he held out his arms. The moisture had stimulated John's yeast and the fragrance of rising dough began to reach the crowd on the bridge. They saw John take another step forward and slowly enfold the angry man's stiff form in an embrace. The two stood there for a moment, and then, to the onlookers' surprise, the angry man reached up with his arms and returned the hug. Then his body started to shake with sobs. The yellow man held him tenderly until his body relaxed and he was still.

The crowd, some fifty strong now, representing all the various constituencies that grace a big old northeastern city, began to clap. The older fisherman, who had been there when the congressman arrived, let out a cheer. His companion wiped his eyes. People shouted: "You go, man!" "Love wins!" "Hurray!" They kept on clapping. The congressman unclasped his arms from around John Dough's middle, turned toward the crowd, and waved. It was still raining, he was still crying. He smiled a shy smile and waved again. The crowd went wild. They clapped and stomped and hollered. "Keep the love going!" "LOVE! LOVE! LOVE!" "City of Brotherly Love!"

THAT NIGHT JOHN Dough and the congressman stayed up late talking in their room on the third floor. Buddy could tell that the congressman was confiding some long-held secrets, so he tactfully left his post by the bathroom door and went to sleep downstairs. He knew that the congressman wouldn't try to run away tonight. Later, he heard the sound of John and the congressman laughing uproariously. He curled up into a contented ball and went back to sleep.

When Philadelphia woke up the next morning to a clear blue sky and a world refreshed by rain, John was already flying the congressman back to Iowa.

16. THE FIFTH KINGDOM

NOT LONG AFTER HIS RETURN FROM THE MIDWEST, JOHN WAS looking out the kitchen window into Alida's back yard and worrying about everything he still had to accomplish. He couldn't regret the time they had spent on the congressman. He was sure, without being able to articulate why, that every single person's happiness was of infinite importance. But it *had* taken a long time, and he and his accomplices were no closer to achieving their most urgent objectives: freeing the country from the ever-present dangers of the Trump administration, introducing crucial legislation, reorienting the American people toward the principles that made America worth preserving. John couldn't help but wonder whether he was up to the job. He was just a dough man of uncertain provenance. Maybe the conspirators' whole enterprise was pitifully unrealistic.

And then, in general, John had accepted the circumstances in which he found himself without dwelling on their apparent implausibility, but sometimes it all seemed disconcertingly fantastic: this spirited, generous older woman and her civic-minded dog—the two of them so intelligent and with such noble aspirations—they seemed like something out of a story! Was this all a dream?

As he stood, weighed down by these misgivings and by the ugly menace that hovered over the country, he caught sight of an unfamiliar shape in the middle of Alida's tiny lawn. It was something like a miniature umbrella, but with a fat handle and a very substantial top.

It was yellow and brown like a popover or a bun. John went upstairs to Alida's study to ask her about it.

"It sounds like a mushroom," she said, looking up from her letter. "They often come up after the rain. There," she added, pointing toward the shelf where she kept her nature books. "Get down that green book called *The Fifth Kingdom*. Maybe you can find out what kind it is."

John took down the book and began to read:

"'According to the Linnaean system of classification, the Fifth Kingdom is the kingdom of fungi and includes mushrooms, molds and yeasts.' Alida!" John exclaimed. "*I* am a member of the Fifth Kingdom!"

"Yes, I guess you are," she said.

John turned to the section of the book that had colored pictures of mushrooms and concluded that the mushroom in the yard was some kind of Boletus. If he was right, the bottom of the mushroom's cap should look like a sponge instead of having little slats called 'gills.' John went down to have a closer look. As he stepped out the back door and onto the grass, the mushroom surprised him by speaking.

"*Servus,** John Dough. Good morning," it said, inclining its cap in greeting. "I have come from the Fifth Kingdom. I have a message for you from *Strobilomyces Floccopus Princeps*."

John Dough bowed in return and said "Hello," before asking, "Please tell me—I'm sorry I don't know—Who's Stro.... ?"

"That's Latin for 'Woolly Mushroom that looks like a Pinecone'; but everyone calls him 'The Old Man of the Woods'. He's the president of the Fifth Kingdom, our *Princeps Fungorum*, ('First Fungus')" replied the Mushroom. "The Fifth Kingdom hasn't been a monarchy for a long time," he explained, "and Latin is no longer our official language—except in government titles and things like that.

---

* I am your servant.

"But before I give you the princeps's message, I have another item of business. I'm sure you know that you were a foundling? Do you still have the token that your adoptive mother found around your neck?"

"I do!" replied John. "Shall I get it?"

"Please," said the mushroom. "Bring it here and I'll show you something."

John hurried back with the token and held it out.

"Excellent!" the other exclaimed warmly. "Here, take this missing piece," and he handed John a little triangular piece of silver. John saw that it fit perfectly into the gap in his token.

"Let me introduce myself," the mushroom went on. "I am *Boletus Legativus*, 'a Bolete of the Foreign Service'. Please call me Bo."

The Boletus's manner conveyed genuine warmth, as well as the confident affability of a successful diplomat. John liked him.

"I'm happy to meet you," he said. "I'm also full of suspense. Can you tell me about my origins?"

"I can!" the mushroom replied. "Our princeps, The Old Man of the Woods, has been deeply concerned for the safety of the forests under the current administration in Washington. It was he that dispatched heroic yeast spores to Alida's kitchen. Delivery spores brought the token to mark you as a hero and to educate Alida about your care."

"How did you choose Alida? How did you know about her?" asked the dough man eagerly.

"Oh, the Fifth Kingdom has a very extensive intelligence system," the Boletus replied. "The mold on the cheddar in the back of Alida's refrigerator is an agent and also the mildew on her garden hose. Yeast spores have broad access throughout the city. Alida is known for her bread baking, her knowledge of mushrooms, and her courage. In addition, she loves the woods. And Buddy, who came to our attention because of Alida, is not only a loyal and high-minded canine; he is a political genius. Oh, the princeps knew where to send his hero!"

"His hero!" John savored the words. If he had really been sent to do this job, he would do it with more confidence. They trusted him. He would rise to the occasion. And the lurking feeling that there was something fabulous or unreal about his associates and the circumstances in which he found himself had finally been removed. He was connected to the Fifth Kingdom in all its earthy reality and unquestionable authority, and the *Princeps Fungorum* himself had recognized Buddy and Alida for their special virtues. Everything made sense now. This wasn't a dream.

The Boletus placed a small kind hand on the hero's foot (which was all he could reach, even though John was crouching) before continuing.

"The Old Man of the Woods would like you to come to his residence in Western Pennsylvania. He has an idea about what you can do with Trump and his henchmen after you remove them from the White House."

"That has been a puzzle for us," John admitted. "In the past I've used trees, but it's not a permanent solution."

The boletus's manner conveyed genuine warmth as well as the confident affability of a successful diplomat.

Bo Legativus gave John careful directions to an ancient forest on the other side of the Appalachians and then—with a few words of heartfelt encouragement—sank back into the earth and was gone.

When Alida came down a little later to look at John's discovery, she just said, "That's the way with mushrooms. They come and they go."

17. THE OLD MAN OF THE WOODS

I looked behind him in the woods
And back again.
As though, I thought, if I just whispered "Whence?"
He might in courtly fashion lift his cap,
And indicate with rural cadence "Yonder."

JOHN WASHED HIS PATCHWORK CAPE IN THE BATHTUB AND
asked Alida to iron it for him. Then he flew out of Philadelphia early
the next morning looking fresh and clean for his meeting with the
leader of the fungal world. He headed out over the suburb of Bala
Cynwyd and continued west.

He alighted on the edge of a forest where pines and beeches,
oaks and sycamores, though massive with age, as Bo had promised
him, were decked out in the tender green of the youngest spring.
Below John's feet the earth was dark and rich or covered with bright
velvety mosses. He sensed that he was in a place alive with fungal
spores of all kinds. Sure enough, he soon started to hear their music.
It was the country music that mushrooms have danced to since their
first appearance in the living world, simple but melodious with some
instrument that was very low like a bassoon and some instrument
that was very high like a reedy piccolo. Through it all was the breezy
undulation of a rustic harp. John followed the music until he arrived
at an American chestnut tree as broad as a tower and at least four

hundred years old. Beneath it on a mossy carpet, solitary and venerable, stood a shaggy brown mushroom—the Old Man of the Woods himself. John bowed, and the Princeps of the Fifth Kingdom bowed courteously back in return.

"Welcome, John Dough!" said the princeps gesturing for his visitor to sit down on the moss with him. Then he waved one of his little hands and the music of the spore orchestra subsided, replaced by the ordinary woodland sounds.

"It lifts my spirits to see you looking so well and so strong," said the mushroom. "I can tell that Alida has tended you well."

"She has!" said John.

"I asked you to come here because I have some information that I thought would be useful to you in your mission. I also wanted to express my gratitude to you and to wish you well."

"Thank you," murmured the young dough hero.

"First the information. I have an idea where you should take the president when he leaves the White House. Where would he go willingly and want to stay? It can't be somewhere where he could do more harm. He needs comfort, pleasure, adulation, and lots of golf. Have you heard," the mushroom asked, "of the Land of the Plant People?"

John shook his head.

"The Plants are an ancient people, mentioned by Aristotle," the princeps explained. "Their country is a lush green land of pleasure, beautiful, expansive, perpetually spring. It rains only at night. There are verdant plains suitable for golf links and ample wetlands suitable for Trump's associates—swamp habitat, you understand. All these things contribute, but what make it a perfect permanent residence for Donald Trump are its inhabitants. They would adore him."

John looked surprised.

"The Plant People," the mushroom explained, "are completely unregulated by rational consistency. Their thoughts and utterances are guided only by impulsive desires for pleasure and prestige. (They call this 'Freedom of Speech'!) The law of Non-contradiction is explicitly outlawed by Article One of their constitution—though, it is true, Article Five insists upon its strict enforcement. Given their particular limitations, the Plants depend upon centralized top-down rule. They have no hang-ups about liberty, which seems to be essentially connected to the possibility of coherent thought.

"All of this is possible, of course, only because the landscape takes care of itself and provides everything the inhabitants need to live in luxury and plenty. *They toil not, neither do they spin,* yet they are always well dressed and in perfect health.

"Finally, they would feel that a human king brought them real prestige. For, although profoundly self-satisfied, the Plant People sense that human beings have some capacity they lack. But, what other human king could they stand? Normal human scruples about consistency are mystifying and infuriating to them. Yes, Donald Trump is perfect for them in every way."

"Where is this Land?" asked John.

"It's in the Garden State," replied the wise old mushroom. "Exit 19 off the New Jersey Turnpike. It's not well marked, but you can find it, if you know it's there."

The princeps paused now and looked at John with a new expression on his face.

"Your dough makes you strong and sweet—" he said after a moment, "gives you the ability to fly and change your shape. But it won't last forever. One of these days, your dough will just rise too high and collapse. This lends some urgency to your work."

John Dough was quiet for a moment, thinking about this new piece of information.

"I should have moved faster," he said.

"Oh, no!" said the mushroom kindly. "You had to prepare yourself for your labors. Heroes never have much time. It's part of their nature."

"How will I know....?" asked John.

The Old Man of the Woods explained to John how he would know when his time was almost up. In the meantime, he should just work fast. He was racing against the clock now.

"Here, let me tuck some messenger spores into the hem of your cape, so that you can reach me quickly if you ever need help or advice," the princeps concluded, and he tucked the spores into the hem of John's cape with his little fungal fingers and taught him the ancient dispatching verse.

Then the music started again and John and the Princeps Fungorum danced together on the soft ground under the towering trees: The Dance of the Departing Hero. When it was over, John bowed again before flying back east to the city.

He danced the Dance of the Departing Hero.

18. BUDDY AND LARRY

WHEN JOHN GOT HOME, BUDDY AND LARRY THE CAT WERE lying on the porch, deep in conversation. This was now a familiar sight. For several days, Alida had been picking Larry up and bringing him over, but Larry had soon decided to move to Strawbridge Street for a while. It was a shame to make his family worry, but bigger things were at stake.

Larry and Buddy were hard at work on Item Two of the conspirators' to-do list: "Health Care, Jobs, Immigration, Clean Energy, Environment, Education: put sound policies in place." There was a lot to iron out between the Republican and the Democrat, but they were gradually charting out a compelling legislative path for America. They had never been happier in their lives.

Buddy enjoyed Larry's casual use of bad language. He found it exotic and funny and expressive of his new friend's whole interesting person. Larry, for his part, was completely smitten by Buddy and his whole family. They reminded him of a forties movie, something with Jimmy Stewart or Gary Cooper: one of those movies where the hero is so wholesome and idealistic that he seems dumb at first, but then it turns out that he's really smart too, and in the end the baddies just can't stomach being bad any more. Buddy and John and Alida—Larry had never met anyone so nice before.

Buddy had been dictating his and Larry's conclusions to John, who typed them up on Alida's computer. They had been making use of the Congressional Research Service and various think-tanks: Brookings Institution, Rand, Center for American Progress, Hoover Institute. John had also helped them to request assorted governmental transcripts through the Freedom of Information Act.

His mind still full of the ancient forest and the Old Man of the Woods, John reclined on the porch swing for a minute and listened to his friends' deliberations. They were discussing the impact on small farms of federally subsidized crop insurance. Suddenly Larry hissed with disgust.

"Buddy, we're idiots! What the fuck do we think we're doing?! Two jerks from the Greater Philadelphia area trying to come up with legislation for the whole country!"

"Hold on!" said Buddy, "You and I have very different perspectives . . . and we can get the information we need online—we really can!" Larry just looked at Buddy, who went on, "We're not only from different parties, we're from different species, and ones whose interests aren't traditionally aligned. . . . "

Larry felt sorry for his friend. He spoke more gently. "Look, Buddy, you've been doing a fantastic job. Honestly, I'm convinced that you're a genius. But think about it: we're both guys from the Northeast. There's stuff we won't think of. You can see that."

Buddy's head sank between his paws. Larry was right, of course. He felt like a fool. He had been blinded by his own excitement. He licked his paws with stunned chagrin. For several minutes the only sound was the thumping of Larry's tail on the porch floor.

19. NO MORE DIY

JOHN GOT UP FROM WHERE HE WAS LYING AND WALKED TO the narrow strip of grass that constituted Alida's front yard. Without explanation, he shook his cape to loosen some of the messenger spores in its hem and said the words that The Old Man of the Woods had taught him:

> *Messengers, away and fly*
> *Through the corridors of sky!*
> *Heed your ancient kingdom's cry:*
> *Sporrò, Sporrò, Sporrò! Tis I!*

The Princeps had urged John to ask for help if he needed it, and he did need it.

After just a few minutes, Bo Legativus poked up from the ground a few feet away. Buddy let out one surprised bark and then shrugged. Nothing really mattered anymore. He and Larry listened with gloomy and apathetic embarrassment as John described their predicament to this odd stranger. Bo listened carefully.

"I have no doubt," he said in a measured tone, full of modest authority, "that creative and astute creatures from all fifty states can be found in a hurry. They must be deeply versed in public policy and genuinely patriotic. Otherwise, there's no way a group with such diverse interests could reach agreement. And, I suppose," he added thoughtfully, "they must be winged creatures, who can get to Philadelphia on their own: birds and insects."

He and John chose a meeting day two weeks away and designated a spot in the park that provided field, forest, and water, in convenient proximity. Only when everything was settled did Bo look up at Buddy and Larry, where they stood on the edge of the porch, and incline his cap respectfully.

"What an honor to meet you both," he said. "Please let me know in the future, if I can help in any way." He then smiled warmly at John, waved a small hand, and sank back into the earth.

Buddy and Larry looked at each other in disbelief. They realized now that they had resources at their disposal beyond their wildest dreams. They felt as though they had been trying to make a movie on their smart phones, and Steven Spielberg or Martin Scorsese had shown up unexpectedly with a complete crew and offered to help. This wasn't DIY any more. Their eyes widened. Larry grinned.

"WILL THE BIRDS be a problem for you?" Buddy asked Larry later.

"No problem there," Larry replied truthfully, without taking offense. "I'm strictly a cat food guy."

20. THE DELEGATES

I could not count or name the multitude who came to
Troy, though I had ten tongues and a tireless voice, and
lungs of bronze as well, if you Olympian Muses, daughters
of aegis-bearing Zeus, brought them not to mind.
—HOMER

BUDDY AND LARRY, ALIDA, AND JOHN ARRIVED AT THE HIGH
Meadow in Fairmount Park before dawn on the appointed morning and waited in the dew-drenched field. It was cool with a hint of rain in the air. Buddy and Larry were quiet, absorbed by a solemn expectancy. Alida, who was a birder, had her binoculars. As the sky lightened, a speck appeared in the distance. They watched as it grew bigger.

Up in the sky, an osprey first spotted the four tiny figures where they stood in the field and called back to the jay behind him: "That must be them!" They passed the message back through the flock to the beat of their tired wings: "That's them!" "That's them!" "That's them!" They had flown all this last night to avoid attention. Most of them had been flying for days, many for longer. The flock had grown bigger as they travelled across the country—each new delegate a cause for renewed excitement. Now they were almost a hundred strong, not counting some of the insects' friends and relations. And they were about to meet the brilliant dog and cat who had gotten all this started.

The flock drew closer and closer. Larry stood very still, alert in every fiber of his being. Buddy wagged his tail more and more vigorously.

Alida lowered her binoculars. The flock was upon them: wings, avian bodies, ruckus and commotion. Birds and insects settled noisily in the trees and in the field, breaking out in morning song or exclamations of greeting and arrival. A loon from Minnesota, who had landed on the pond at the bottom of the hill, filled the woods with her lingering call, causing several people with houses near the park to dream of northern lakes.

Alida, lips parted in excitement, trained her binoculars on a mountain bluebird in a red oak who was conversing with an olive colored warbler. A kite from Utah had already launched into his views on military spending to a mixed group in a sugar maple. It's hard to do justice to the diversity and beauty, the sense of purpose, the excited patriotism that belonged to this assemblage.

When John Dough stepped out into the field to address the company, everyone fell silent. He held out his arms and turned to indicate the whole congress. He smiled his warm intelligent smile.

"Welcome! Welcome to all!" he said. "Rest where you are. A group of delegates who didn't have to travel far will come to you to discuss committees. Buddy and Larry, the delegates from Pennsylvania," he indicated his friends with a gesture, "will be stationed here to answer questions and receive suggestions." A cardinal from Delaware flew down to the pond to relay John's message to the water birds.

And so, the Continental Congress of 2017, without further ceremony, began its historic work. Maybe you are wondering: how could such a disparate group with such varying interests come to agree on constructive legislation for the whole United States? Cooperation and creativity of that kind are always something of a miracle;

but remember that these delegates were picked from the whole winged population of the United States for their special political genius and their absolute commitment to the health and prosperity of the nation. True patriotism, after all, is a kind of love and therefore shares in love's creative power. In this atmosphere, a mourning dove could serve safely on a committee with a red-tailed hawk, a mother Carey's chicken from Maine could be trusted to listen to the concerns of a hornet from Detroit. There's nothing more conducive to a Peaceable Kingdom than shared devotion to a common goal.

John's main job was to act as a sort of reference librarian and scribe, providing documents and resources of all kinds, and committing the delegates' conclusions to writing. This he did with superheroic speed. Somehow John would have to deliver to the US Congress the massive packet of policy suggestions that the delegates produced. But that was in the future. Now the task for John was just to facilitate the delegates in their creative work. Alida served as a caterer, providing a varied menu to accommodate every dietary taste and restriction. Feeding the pelican was her favorite chore of the day.

ALTHOUGH THE BIRDS did their best to stay discreetly out of sight, ornithologists across the country, who were used to receiving calls from friends in other fields asking them to identify birds (not very precisely described), were suddenly swamped with inquiries from Philadelphia. They had to stop answering their phones.

PART

THREE

21. JOHN DOUGH GOES TO WASHINGTON

WHEN THE LEAVES WERE FULLY OUT ON THE TREES AND THE delegates' work was almost done, John decided to go to Washington. The situation was urgent. Trump was continuing to encourage white supremacists, and people were getting killed. He was threatening nuclear war on twitter. And John knew that his dough couldn't last much longer. It was time to get the president to the Land of the Plant People.

The air space over the nation's capitol was too closely monitored for flying, so John took the train. He had plenty to think about on the ride. His plan depended on speaking to Donald Trump in private, but he still didn't know how he was going to pull it off. Ingress and egress were not a problem for him. He could always get through fences, gates, and doors, by squeezing through bit by bit. The challenge was to avoid being seen and stopped. Even a puddle of dough, he reflected, would be conspicuous. He couldn't go at night, though, because then there would be alarms set everywhere. Well, he could better assess obstacles and opportunities when he got there; now he should familiarize himself with the layout of the White House building and grounds. He found a good map online.

It was a beautiful May morning in the capitol. John took the Metro to Federal Triangle and then strolled over to the White House on E St. He walked along the fence until he got to a place where a police car was parked right next to the sidewalk. Two policemen were standing on the sidewalk in front of it. They were relaxed. This was evidently part of their regular beat. John stopped not too far from them and looked through the fence at the White House. He figured that it was better to know exactly who was watching him than to be spotted from a distance. The policemen, who were experienced officers, weren't interested in John: his body language was innocent and his get-up wasn't surprising—not in this town. They chatted about plans to increase security on this side of the White House and the NFL draft.

As John stood gazing through the fence, he saw three young squirrels (teenagers, he supposed) rough-housing on the White House lawn under a small maple. They chased each other across the grass and up and down the trunk of the tree. They jumped on each other's backs and rolled around; they wrestled with their forepaws. Every once in a while, they stopped to groom themselves or each other with their little teeth. It wasn't always clear whether they were playing or quarrelling. One of them caught sight of John and ran over, stopping a few yards away to stare.

"Hello," said John.

"Hi," said the squirrel. He came a little closer and looked at John again before adding, "You smell good. What are you made of?"

"Bun dough," answered John.

"Cool," said the squirrel.

"What are you three up to?"

"Bored out of our minds," answered the squirrel. The other two squirrels had come a little closer now and were staring at John. "That's my sister and our friend," he added.

"I could use some help," said John.

"What are you trying to do?" asked the squirrel.

"I'm trying to get through the fence without being seen," answered John.

"Like this?" said the squirrel and he ran back and forth through the fence. The other two squirrels came closer.

"I can get through easily too, because I'm made of dough," said John, "but people would notice me."

"How come you don't want to be noticed?" asked the squirrel.

"I want to talk to the president in his office, but hardly anyone's allowed in, and I don't have an appointment."

"Do you like the new president?" asked the squirrel.

"No," said John honestly. (The squirrel hadn't been asking about sentiments of universal goodwill.)

"Well, at least he doesn't have a dog," answered the squirrel. "The last president had two."

"That's true," said John.

"Do you have a plan?" asked the squirrel.

"Well, I was thinking that if someone created a distraction, I might be able to slip through the fence very quickly without being seen and then, as soon as I got to the other side, I'd pretend to be a statue of George Washington."

"Wouldn't they notice a statue popping up all of a sudden?" asked the squirrel's sister, who had now joined them.

"There are so many statues of Washington in Washington," explained John, "that I don't think anyone really notices them anymore."

"But you don't look like Washington," she persevered.

"Oh, I can change my shape," explained John.

"Then what would you do after that?" asked the third squirrel, who had come up too.

"I'd hope for some kind of helpful development," said John.

"That doesn't sound like a great plan," said the girl.

"Don't listen to Shevawn," the first squirrel said. "She's always a downer."

"I am not!" said Shevawn. "I just think he's gonna get shot."

"We've seen stuff," said the third squirrel impressively.

"Well, as far as creating a distraction for you," said the first squirrel, whose name was Danny, "we'd have to do something pretty interesting for it to work, because people don't notice squirrels. I mean, it's good for us, because we can go wherever we want." And he went back and forth through the fence again, swishing his tail and laughing in an exaggerated and provocative way. "See? They don't even care. But," he went on thoughtfully, sitting back on his haunches and rubbing his ear with his paw, "what if instead of just running by screaming or something, we act out a little drama? That might hold their attention."

"A cop drama," said Shevawn excitedly. "That'd interest them."

"I'm in," said the third squirrel, whose name was Nate.

JOHN GOT OUT his cell phone and pretended to have a long tedious business conversation, so that the policemen wouldn't wonder why he was standing there so long. He leaned casually against the fence. "No, that's okay, I can wait.... If you could just ask Carl to look it up.... It should be under 'Schmidt'.... No, please, take your time." Behind him he could hear the squirrels preparing.

"Just because I'm a girl, I have to play the victim?!"

"It's because you're so pretty," said Nate. "They'll sympathize with you."

"I'll be either the crook or the cop," said Shevawn. "That's it!"

It was a long process.

EVENTUALLY JOHN SAW Nate coming through the fence and out onto the sidewalk. He picked up a piece of powdered jelly doughnut lying by the curb and walked to a spot about five feet directly in front of the cops. He held the doughnut in his front paws and started to nibble at it.

"Look," said the taller cop. "That's cute."

"Mmhm," said his colleague looking over and then looking away again.

Then Shevawn let out a sort of shriek from the fence. Both cops looked over. She bared her teeth and walked deliberately toward Nate. They watched her circle him slowly and then pounce, throwing him to the ground and grabbing the doughnut. She walked about a foot away from him and then held up the doughnut and pranced around in place on her hind legs, unmistakably gloating. Nate twitched his tail and held his head with his paws in anger and despair. At that moment Danny entered stage right chattering very loudly and angrily. He stormed over to Shevawn and bit her tail. She squealed and dropped the doughnut. Danny picked it up and carried it over to Nate, who took it from him. Nate hugged it to his chest in his forepaws as though rejoicing. Danny then turned and chased Shevawn back through the fence. The cops clapped. They were pleased to see justice prevail. Nate stuffed the doughnut into his mouth, so that his cheeks bulged, and ran after his friends.

The cops looked after them and then the shorter one said,

"I don't remember that statue of George Washington over there. Has it always been there?"

"There are so many statues of Washington all over the District that I don't really notice them anymore. But I think that one's new. They must have moved it from somewhere."

"WOW! THAT REALLY worked," said Danny.

"Yeah, but what's he going to do now?" said Shevawn. "He's stuck there."

"Shevawn, you're a really good actress, " said Nate.

John didn't dare say anything. He had to stay perfectly still. The cops were looking at him and he heard voices approaching. It sounded like a tour. The voices got louder and soon he was surrounded by a group of about fifteen tourists.

"I haven't seen this statue before," said the tour guide, but it's clearly based on the famous portrait by Charles Willson Peale: Washington at the Battle of Princeton, commissioned by the Executive Council of Pennsylvania in 1779."

"Look, it's got a little patchwork cape," said a tourist.

The tour guide sighed. He hadn't noticed that. Somewhere there would be an earnest explanation by the artist of the function that the cape played in his or her "piece:" something about the conversation between American folk art and the political establishment represented by Washington. He wasn't making fun of anyone. He just wished that spin weren't always such a big part of art these days. Or maybe the cape was just meant to be silly and fun, like covering tree trunks and parking meters with little knitted sweaters. What was it called? "Tree bombing?" It was innocent enough, but that bothered him too. It wasn't that he didn't have a sense of humor, but it seemed to him that there was something deficient in a sensibility that could only produce or appreciate silly incongruities.

"Well, on to the Rose Garden now!" he said turning, and all the tourists followed him.

"OMG!" SAID SHEVAWN. "He went with them!"

Sure enough, John Dough, no longer looking like Washington, was following along at the back of the group.

"We better go too, in case he needs help," said Danny, "Besides, I wanna see what happens!"

The three squirrels ran to catch up.

22. HEROISM IN THE ROSE GARDEN

ONCE IN THE ROSE GARDEN, JOHN FROZE AGAIN AND ASSUMED his disguise. The group noticed him when they moved on a little bit to look at the tulips.

"Look, there's another one!" said one of the tourists.

The tour guide saw that there was indeed another statue of Washington identical to the first, erected there by a crab apple tree, and this one also had a patchwork cape. I see, he thought, it's a whole thing: like one of those initiatives where they fill the shopping district of some town with statues of bears or mules or something—variously decorated—to make the place seem happening. He continued describing Jefferson's architectural innovations.

The squirrels noticed that, every time John thought that the attention of the tour was elsewhere, he would move slowly toward the French doors of the Oval Office. They watched enthralled. It was like a game that they had played when they were little: *Red Light, Green Light.*

The tour guide turned sideways and gestured at the West Colonnade behind him, and the group all looked where he was pointing. "Green light," thought Shevawn, and she watched John Dough take two little steps. The tour guide adjusted his position again. "Red light!" shouted Shevawn in her head, and she saw John Dough freeze.

"To the right you can see where the Kennedys. . . ."

Green light! John took three steps toward the French doors. "To the left...."

Red light! John froze.

By this method the dough man had made quite a bit of progress toward his destination, when something went wrong. The whole crowd had their backs turned, and John was taking advantage of the opportunity to cover more ground than usual, when the tour guide suddenly spun around. He had been telling a little known story about the flock of sheep that President Wilson brought in to graze the White House lawn during World War 1 and was acting out the part where Mrs. Wilson spins around to see a sheep charging at her and the Swedish Ambassador's wife. "Oh, RED LIGHT! RED LIGHT! RED LIGHT!" mouthed Shevawn desperately, holding her head with her paws. John froze, but it was too late. The tour guide had seen him moving and the look of astonishment on his face was unmistakable. Shevawn shrieked. She ran straight at the tour guide and ran right up his pant leg. That got everyone's attention.

"Shevawn!" cried Nate in anguish, but Danny, who was a quick thinker like his sister, sprinted at the group chattering. Shevawn leapt to the ground from the tour guide's shoulder, and all three squirrels ran as fast as they could back to their maple. The doubly astonished tour guide watched them run away and then turned back to the moving statue, but it was gone. He

It's okay! I saw. He got away!

looked around, took a deep breath and guided his little flock toward the safety of the West Wing.

Effectively hidden by a low box hedge, not far from the French door into the Oval Office, was a long deep puddle of dough breathing deeply. Nearby, and equally well hidden, was a patchwork cape. The puddle waited a good five minutes in its hiding place before creeping up to the French window and moving particle by gooey particle under the closed door.

BACK AT THE maple Shevawn was crying. Nate rubbed his head against her fur.

"It's okay," he said. "I saw. He got away."

23. THE OVAL OFFICE

IF DONALD TRUMP HAD BEEN A CRIER, HE WOULD HAVE CRIED that afternoon. He was the most mistreated man on the face of the earth—mistreated and misunderstood. He went over in his mind all the people and institutions that were giving him a hard time:

the press
the courts
the FBI
the CIA
the DOJ
America's allies
America's enemies
Democrats
more and more Republicans
77% of the American people

Even the country's laws were out to get him. You couldn't do a thing without encountering some trivial objection. And then there was this Russian thing. God knows where it would end. It was starting to make him feel very uncomfortable. He let his head fall to his desk. He had been up much of the night communicating with the world on social media and he was tired.

As soon as Donald fell asleep, his gloomy thoughts were replaced by nice ones. He dreamt that he was at a party in New York—no, not in New York, somewhere in Russia, and there were gold tables, and the tables were singing something very festive: that Lou Bega song about the girls. As the tables sang, the wine glasses pranced around on the table as though they were the girls in the refrain:

A little bit of Monica in my life
A little bit of Erica by my side
A little bit of Rita is all I need. . . .

It was lots of fun and Donald was laughing. He looked over at the next table happily and expectantly, as though to say, "Isn't this a lot of fun?" and met the unsmiling gaze of Angela Merkel. She was sitting with Obama and that new guy with the dour face and the gray hair who was investigating him. They were all looking at him in an unfriendly, inflexible way. The music stopped. Donald groaned. Even in his dream, it all came back to him: the difficult position he was in, the viciousness of the press, the unreliability of officials in every branch of government. At that moment Ambassador Kislyak put his doughy hand on Trump's shoulder and said sincerely, "There's a way out, Donald." Donald looked up gratefully, but it wasn't Kislyak, after all. The face was kinder and more trustworthy—without Kislyak's grin. It was looking at him with genuine sympathy. He put his hand up over the soft hand on his shoulder. He would have sniffed, had he been a crier. He was in the Oval Office now. He must have been dreaming, but now he was awake. He turned and looked at the doughy man, who was not Kislyak.

"Who are you?" he asked.

"I came to help," answered John simply, moving so that he was facing the president. "My name is John Dough."

The name was familiar to Donald, but he didn't know where he had heard it before.

"Can you help?" he asked.

"I can," said John. "Everything's going to be all right."

Again Donald had the feeling he would have sniffed, had he been that kind of person. Could everything really be all right? For some time he had been feeling that nothing would ever be all right again. There were good times occasionally, like when he was with the Saudis, or when he crashed a wedding at one of his golf clubs and everyone was glad to see him, but more and more the future seemed threatening and the present oppressive.

"Everything you try to do," the president said to John, "someone gets in your way. The Senate, the House, judges—even judges! Who could have known that some judge somewhere. . . ? And then the press. . . . They are so bad; I mean really bad. And they're allowed to . . . just write stuff about you . . . I mean really nasty stuff. It's so unfair. I don't understand," he said lowering his voice, "why I'm not allowed to do something about them. Other leaders get to. . . . Erdogan told me. . . . and Duterte. . . . But here it's like anything goes!"

John listened with his observant and sympathetic gaze. The president liked this doughy man and he could tell that the doughy man liked him. The doughy man understood how hard everything was; he didn't blame him. Donald was right about that part: John didn't blame him. What did Alida say? "Some have a greater measure of light"? Donald Trump had just been allotted a very small measure, a scant pinch. Endowed, as he was, with so very scant a measure, he had to be gotten out of the White House as fast as possible, but John didn't blame him. Who could discern and interpret the intricate web of causation that had produced Donald Trump's mind and accurately apportion blame? In fact, John felt a pity for Donald that the president could not have imagined, let alone understood.

"You shouldn't be president," said John. "Presidents are supposed to preserve and protect. You should be king. You would make a great king."

Donald looked up interested.

"You know, " he said, "I would. I would make a great king." But then he had a sudden misgiving: "I couldn't do a beard though—no way—so maybe not."

"A beard isn't necessary," said John. "There are many different kinds of kings. No other president in history has been as fit to be king as you are—a certain kind of king. Have you heard of Tarquinius Superbus, the last king of Rome? Well, never mind. A democracy doesn't really suit you. In a democracy there is an inevitable preoccupation with truth and consistency."

"Consistency? I like things with a smooth consistency."

"Exactly," said John Dough. "If you were king everything would go smoothly for you."

"It's too bad you can't be king anymore," said Donald.

"But you can!" said John. "There's a kingdom right nearby that needs a king. I can't imagine anyone who would do a better job than you."

"King Donald," said the president musingly. "What's the name of the country?"

"It's called the Land of the Plant People. But you could rebrand . . . Trumplandia? That has a ring to it. They would love you there," he added.

"They would love me?"

"They would *adore* you!" said John.

"But, *Plant* People?" said Trump skeptically. "I'm not that keen on nature."

"Oh, these are very unnatural plants," John reassured him. "And famous. Aristotle mentioned them, you know."

"The Greek guy?" asked Donald.

"Yes, exactly," said John, surprised by this display of erudition on the President's part.

"Billionaire who married Jackie K.? He liked the place?"

"What's amazing is that there should be acreage like that so close to The City!" answered John, changing the subject. Buddy had told him about how New Yorkers talked about 'The City', and he felt that this was one of the situations in which they might say it.

"Very rich guys can always get classy women. That's a good example: how Aristotle got Jackie K. Didn't matter he was Greek!" He paused for a moment before asking with a sudden frown: "And the Russian stuff?"

"You would just leave it behind! The Plant People couldn't care less about that kind of thing."

"I was clever you know. I was smart."

"Of course, you were," said John. "And now it would be smart for you to get out of here."

"Could I bring my people with me?"

"Absolutely. You could insist upon it and no one would disagree. You should bring everyone who's been loyal to you. It would be a very popular move."

At that moment one of the telephones on the President's desk buzzed discreetly. He looked over sharply, hesitated, and then walked over and picked it up. On his face was a hunted expression.

"No!" he said. "I'm busy. I can't—"

There was a tap on the door.

"They never listen!" said the President petulantly.

The Chief of Staff opened the door to the Oval Office.

"Sir . . . " he said, taking a step in, "It's very important that. . . . "
There was a new life-size statue of George Washington standing right in front of the President's desk. God! Why couldn't things just be normal?

The president turned red. "YOU GET THE FUCK OUT OF HERE!" he yelled.

"Sir—"

"Or YOU'RE FIRED!"

The Chief of Staff, not particularly surprised, left to get reinforcements.

"You have to talk to them that way," the president said, turning apologetically to John, who had relaxed into his normal shape again. "It's the only thing they understand."

24. SECOND THOUGHTS

"IT'S OUT, JOHN," DONALD SAID. "IT'S IMPOSSIBLE."

"What is, Donald?" asked John.

"Leaving and becoming king. I can't do it."

They were in the residential quarter, with the door locked, packing. Donald had been pointing to things that he wanted to bring with him and John had been fetching them and putting them into two large suitcases.

"Why not?" asked John

"They'll say that I left because I—you know—couldn't hack it."

"Hmm," said John. "How about if you made it clear that you got a better offer?"

"A better offer—you know it! A guy like me doesn't leave unless he gets a better fucking offer! *King* Donald!"

"I have an idea!" said John. "What if you did something that made a splash before you left? Something really important, something that showed that you were really good at being president?"

"That's a great idea!" said Donald, his face brightening. "Like maybe drop a huge bomb on some country that no one likes?"

"Not that!" said John, and then added "Bombs can be tricky. They're almost always unpopular in the end. I know! What about this? What if you left behind a massive packet of policy proposals for Congress? Really brilliant proposals that solved all the country's problems—infrastructure, immigration, health care, jobs, energy? That would be popular with everyone and very impressive. That would make a splash!"

"Yeah," said Donald, pleased. "Yeah, like: 'Here, children, you couldn't figure out what to do, but I could. Here's some stuff for you to work with!' And then I leave it behind like I'm kind of tossing it to them in a sort of this-was-easy-for-me here-you-go way." But then his face fell. "Only thing is: how could I get the packet? I couldn't ask my staff. They're so suspicious. And they probably couldn't do it anyway. You wouldn't believe how slow they are. And it is kind of complicated—coming up with that stuff. Turns out. Complicated and—God!" he said shuddering, "so boring!"

"I could help," said John.

"You could?" asked Donald.

"Sure," said John. "I could get you a packet like that."

"You know some people?" asked Donald.

"I have some friends," said John.

'What would they want in return?"

"Oh, believe me, they have reason to do what I want!" John answered honestly but suggestively, hoping that Donald would supply some reason he could understand.

"Do me a favor? Pack those two shirts on the end." Donald pointed. "Think I'll wear them the first two days as king. And the royal toothbrush," Donald added playfully. "Don't forget the royal toothbrush!"

"YOU KNOW, JOHN," Donald said a little later. He was slumped comfortably in a stuffed arm chair, with his feet outstretched and his hands clasped over his stomach, watching John close up the suitcase. "I'm having second thoughts about bringing all those people with me."

"Uh huh?" said John.

"It could be relaxing to be away from them all. Make a fresh start."

"Oh, I don't think you'd want to leave them behind."

"Why not?" asked Donald.

"Two reasons," said John. "First, you'll need help governing your new country. You don't want to have to find a whole new court."

"That *would* be a pain," Donald agreed.

"And second," continued John, "if you leave them behind, they may feel pressure to kind of distance themselves from you, imply that anything that went wrong was your fault, not theirs."

"They would do that?" Donald asked, and then answered his own question: "Of course, they would! Who wouldn't?"

"Better to bring 'em all along," said John. "Then they can work for you instead of against you."

"But what if they don't want to come? Could happen. You can't trust anyone!"

"Well, in that case," said John. "I would advise you to ask one of your lawyers to draw something up laying out the history of your work with them over the last several years—in very precise language. You can put down anything else you know about them that you think would be useful. Include documents and recordings. Then they won't be tempted to stay behind."

"You know, you're pretty smart," said Donald "for a nice guy."

"Thank you," said John. "Listen, why don't you call your lawyer right away? And I'll call my friends. Let's get everything ready. We're going to have to act fast, if we want to pull this thing off."

"Wait, if I get all this stuff written down though, won't it implicate me?"

"It will make you look as clever as you did for not paying your taxes. And no one can bother you once you're in the Land of the Plant People."

25. AUNT ALIDA

JOHN CALLED HOME.

"Alida, can you put Buddy on the phone?" Alida had perceived pretty early on that her dog was communicating on a sophisticated level with the dough hero, and this fact had, of course, been tacitly acknowledged in connection with the arrival of the delegates and the animals' legislative work, but nevertheless she was surprised by John's request. Now wasn't the time for questions, though. John's voice, courteous as ever, had carried a note of urgency. She left the telephone receiver lying on the rug where Buddy could speak into it and went and fetched the dog.

Buddy confirmed to John that the packet was ready for delivery. Alida had spent the day compiling the documents on her computer—close to a thousand pages—and printed out two copies.

Buddy stopped barking into the receiver and nudged Alida's leg gently with his nose to show her that he was finished on the phone.

"Alida, it's urgent," John explained when she came back. "I don't think I can leave the president's side until I have him safely settled in his new kingdom. The president's bodyguard is ready to meet you at a bar in Foggy Bottom in four hours. Do you think you can find a way to bring the packet here?"

"I'll see and call you right back." Alida was good in an emergency.

Alida's children didn't live nearby, and she no longer drove a car, but that didn't mean that she was without resources. She was very popular with all her young relatives. This afternoon she called one of her great nephews, a young man in his twenties named Ogden.

Ogden was at a barbecue at his vegetable plot in South Philadelphia when his phone rang.

"Aunt Alida?" he said. "Hey! What's up?" He listened to her explanation and then called over to the group at the grill. "Hey guys, my Aunt Alida has to deliver something to a guy in Washington tonight. Anyone wanna come? . . . I don't know. A manuscript of some kind. . . . No, not drugs!"

An outgoing young woman named Rachel, who had met Alida before, said that she wanted to come.

"I've got a ride!" said Alida to John a minute later, and he gave her more detailed instructions.

TRUMP'S BODYGUARD WAS a discreet and loyal man, who was willing to do what his boss required, but this he had felt was—yes—demeaning. An elderly woman with strange clothes and completely uncolored hair, like a homeless person, accompanied by two laughing young people in stained overalls, met him at Pinstripe and handed him a heavy cardboard box (that had evidently once contained IPA), in an earth-stained canvas shopping bag. There was no keeping the bag from touching both his suit and the upholstery of his car. And when he had returned, the president had asked him to fetch a patchwork rag from under a box bush in the Rose Garden. Maybe his boss really was in trouble the way some people said.

(Free from the Bonds of Reason)

26. THE LAND OF THE PLANT PEOPLE

THEY DEPARTED THE NEXT MORNING, BEFORE DAWN, IN THE president's limousine, just John, Donald, his lawyer, and his bodyguard at the wheel.

It was the harried Chief of Staff who first came into the Oval Office, looking for the missing president, and found his note. It was propped up against a stack of envelopes on the president's desk, and addressed "to whom it may concern," in the president's handwriting. He had left—the note stated simply—to become king of the "Land of the Plant People." At first the Chief of Staff thought that it was some kind of joke and he clucked with exasperation, but then he saw the stack of individual letters addressed to Trump's associates, including himself. His own letter—and he assumed the others were like it—was written by the president's lawyer and informed him, in chillingly formal language, about a letter that had already been sent about him to the FBI. Included was an insert providing instructions for catching the buses for the Land of the Plant People later that day, as well as an enticing description of its pleasures. The last item on the desk was a cardboard box of papers addressed simply 'CONGRESS'. As he hurried out of the office, he noticed that the statue of Washington that had appeared yesterday was gone again.

DONALD WAS ENTIRELY happy with The Land of the Plant People, and the Plants, as the Old Man of the Woods had supposed, adored their new king.

Three packed buses departed from the White House later that day. A few passengers were eager to enjoy the amenities of the Land of the Plants, but most of them felt, given the revelations Trump had made about them before he left, that their political prospects would be brighter in another country.

>———⁌———⁌

And very soon they encountered several garrulous carnivorous plants, whose company was not much worse than each other's.

John didn't fly back to Philadelphia until he had seen everyone safely settled.

27. CONGRESS

OF ALL THE SUCCESSORS TO THE PRESIDENT STIPULATED BY the Constitution, only the sixth in the line of succession remained: a widely respected general. He agreed to take over the responsibilities of the Oval Office temporarily, but declined the presidency on the grounds that a civilian chief executive would be more reassuring to the citizenry.

Given the departures of the day before, and the general's laudable scruples, Congress was going to have to choose a new president for the first time in history, and several congressional seats were empty, but this is not what engrossed the lawmakers as they met behind closed doors. They had found the packet addressed to Congress and marked LEGISLATIVE SUGGESTIONS, and they were reading and discussing the contents with the most avid interest. The fact was that whatever group had crafted this legislation—and clearly the ex-president had had nothing to do with it—they were political geniuses of the first water. The solutions were creative, far-reaching, and mutually supporting. They showed a thorough understanding of the needs of the whole country—north, south, east, west, urban, and rural. And the authors had clearly not been mere technicians; on the contrary, they showed the most sensitive awareness of the need to generate and sustain political support among diverse constituencies.

And—incredibly—it was all being given as a present to THEM! Their names would go down in history like the signers of the Constitution! Here, in outline, were plenty of bills to go around. Senators and Representatives camped at the Capitol. The only people they saw were the people delivering their food. A giddy elation and conspiratorial comraderie reigned.

There were no press conferences and not a single leak.

28. THE PRESS: PUZZLES

ONE OF THE BULWARKS OF DEMOCRACY, IN THE FACE OF AN uncommunicative government, is the free press, and journalists were wild to find out what the heck was going on. These were among the lists of things for which they had no explanation:

1. The president, almost all of his cabinet, and several high-ranking congressmen had disappeared. The vehicles in which they were being conveyed had last been spotted on the New Jersey Turnpike but had been subsequently completely lost from sight. There was no video record of them at any of the exits on the Turnpike.

2. The president had left behind a rather incoherent note saying that he was leaving to become king of The Land of the Plant People.

3. He had also left behind a quite coherent record of his associates' involvement in assorted compromising activities. This record had been carefully drawn up by a lawyer (who had also disappeared) and was accompanied by corroborative materials such as recordings, signed agreements, financial documents, texts, and e-mails. Almost all of the

people implicated had departed immediately after the president, including quite a few people who held high positions in the US government.

4. All the remaining congressmen and congresswomen of the United States were holed up in the Capitol buildings. A delivery woman from Pizza World told a reporter for the *Washington Times* that they appeared not only healthy but also, as she had put it, "extremely psyched about something."

5. Probably completely unrelated, but worth mentioning: one of the congressmen of Iowa had been kidnapped some weeks before—according to multiple eye-witness accounts—by a flying creature that smelled of bun dough. The congressman had been missing for five days and claimed not to remember what had happened to him.

While the journalists pondered these questions, the vigilant officers of the Metropolitan Police Department of the District of Columbia were hard at work sifting through footage from surveillance cameras stationed around the White House, and at last, in collaboration with the White House security staff, who had been looking at their own video footage, they identified a person of interest.

29. WEAR IT AS LONG AS YOU CAN

THE CONGRESSMAN FROM IOWA, LIKE ALL OF HIS COLLEAGUES in the House and the Senate, was sleeping in his office in order to facilitate his work on the new legislation. Sleeping on a cot reminded him of his time at Alida's house and was therefore a source of pleasure to him. He had even picked some little white clover on the lawn of his building and put them in a coffee cup on his windowsill, as a small act of piety toward his new friends, in memory of the little bouquet Alida had picked for him. He had also ordered a small rainbow flag online that would some day sit on his desk; but it was still in its cardboard box in his office closet. He wasn't ready to take it out yet. He didn't want to cheapen any of his new feelings and ideas with "outward show." That's what the Quakers called it instead of 'self-promotion' or 'marketing' or 'showing off'—"outward show." The congressman had been reading a little about the Quakers in his spare time in order to better understand his time in Philadelphia. Some of the books were kind of hard going, but there was one that he liked: a biography of William Penn written for children. William Penn was the son of an admiral and converted to Quakerism against his family's wishes. George Fox, the English founder of Quakerism, was kind of an odd guy, the congressman got the impression, but the young William Penn had been really taken with him. Here was the congressman's favorite story. For the story you had to know that the

Quakers were pacifists. (The congressman didn't hold with pacifism himself—but neither did Alida, evidently. He chuckled affectionately remembering how she had shoved him into the water. "What a toughy!" he thought.) Anyway, Penn was a handsome, elegant young man, when he converted, who wore a feather in his hat and a sword at his side. Evidently, he had gone to George Fox and asked him whether he should stop wearing his sword, now that he was a Quaker. Fox had replied, "Wear it as long as you can." That was pretty striking! The idea was that good actions had to spring from your conscience (your inner light), not from an effort to conform to external expectations. The congressman had thought a lot about that: "Wear it as long as you can." He decided that he would keep his little Confederate flag on his office desk as long as he could. It was funny though, after all those years, he found that he really couldn't stand it one second longer. He would have burned it, but it was made of some synthetic material and he was afraid that it would melt in a little puddle under a cloud of toxic fumes, so instead he cut it into tiny pieces with his desk scissors and put the pieces into his congressional wastebasket.

The congressman had woken up that morning feeling happy, as he almost always did these days. He sang a song from his youth, a little tunelessly, as he walked down to the cafeteria for breakfast— *Oh, you can't hurry love. No, you just gotta wait . . .* , and he greeted his sleepy colleagues a little more enthusiastically than they would have wished, given the hour. But the smile died on his lips as he looked down at the morning paper. On the front page were three grainy pictures of John Dough, and a headline that said, "UNIDENTIFIED MAN ON GROUNDS OF WHITE HOUSE DAY BEFORE PRESIDENT'S DISAPPEARANCE." The congressman read the first sentence: "An unidentified man was captured by video surveillance cameras entering the White House grounds on the day before the president's disappearance," and dropped the paper. It was a question of minutes—if it hadn't already happened—before eyewitnesses in Iowa would connect those pictures with the congressman's kidnapper, and someone in Philadelphia would report having seen him there. There must be many people who actually knew where John Dough lived. He was always sitting on the front porch, for God's sake! The congressman grabbed his uneaten breakfast and hurried back to his office.

John must be gotten out of sight and away from Alida's house as quickly as possible. Where could he go? Mary! She would help. Older people are often still listed in Directory Assistance . . . Mary Smith . . . she was! She might well still be home. It was only 7:45. The congressman pressed the buttons of his phone with shaking fingers. She answered the phone. Thank God!

"Mary! This is the congressman."

"Hello," said Mary. "Is everything okay?"

"No. It's about John Dough. It's an emergency."

The congressman explained to Mary what had happened. The two decided that Mary would pick John and Alida up immediately and drive them to her brother's house in Baltimore. That way, John would be hidden, Alida could avoid questioning, and the congressman could come confer with John without too much delay. Mary got right off the phone.

Now the congressman had some thinking to do. John Dough had evidently had a hand in the disappearance of Trump and his associates. Knowing John, the congressman was sure that the whole thing had been accomplished as humanely as possible, but he also supposed that John had used force. And what if some accident had occurred? Maybe he had tried to fly with too many people stuck in his dough or had underestimated the president's weight.

Then a sudden thought made the congressman start: God, they weren't all at Strawbridge Street, were they?! Alida wasn't taking Steve Bannon fishing in the Wissahickon this very minute?! No, no. Mary would have known. But still, the possibilities were truly alarming.

And the legislation: supposedly Trump had left it behind when he departed. Did John Dough and his friends have something to do with that too? It had been inconceivable that anything that good could have emanated from Donald Trump or any of his people. Maybe the legislation was also somehow John Dough's doing. Come to think of it, he remembered having seen the Congressional Research Service up on John's computer. It had struck him at the time, because—the way the dog was sitting—it had looked as though he was reading it. Was it possible that the amazing dough man had written all that stuff? The congressman didn't know what to think. The guy could fly, after all.

30. BALTIMORE

THE CONGRESSMAN HAD BEEN SO INTENT ON HIS MISSION that he hadn't thought about the interpersonal side of the impending reunion. He had asked the cab driver to drop him off about half a mile from his real destination to preserve secrecy, and it was only now, walking through a neighborhood that seemed very much like Alida's, that he thought about seeing them all again. He realized that, after John dropped him off in Iowa, and up until this morning, when he called Mary from his office, he had assumed that he would never see them again, as though they had been funny apparitions sent to him by a loving but quirky god. Mary met him at the door and shook his hand warmly. Her brother was still at work. The others were watching TV.

"You-know-who's on every channel!" she said, smiling. "Come on in."

And then there they all were: John, Alida, and even Buddy! Gosh he was glad to see them! He laughed with pleasure. Alida and John both gave him a hug. Buddy stood up and wagged his tail courteously to show that things between them were on a new footing. The congressman noticed that the orange cat was here too. Mary's brother must be an accommodating guy to take in the animals too.

No time to waste, though.

"John, can we go somewhere and talk? I think the first step is for you just to fill me in."

Mary showed the two into the kitchen and then left, closing the door, so that they could talk without distraction.

"John, I want to help," the congressman began, "but I need to understand the whole situation."

John paused. Honesty was in his yeast, but the congressman didn't know what he was in for.

"You may wish that you didn't know everything," John said. "There are aspects of all this that you may not like."

"John," said the congressman earnestly. He had thought about this question in the cab. "I may be troubled by something you've done, but I want to hear everything. I want to understand and I want to help."

But the congressman had merely supposed that John Dough might have killed someone. He had never imagined that "everything" could include animals with legislative talents and talking mushrooms.

In the back of the congressman's mind had been the idea that maybe John could come to the Capitol. There were a few places where the legislative outlines were obscure or ambiguous. If John were the author, he might be able to provide some really useful clarification. And the lawmakers would have reason to work with the dough man, if, in that way, they could guarantee that they could safely put their names on the final bills, without being exposed as plagiarizers or frauds. But as John told his story, the congressman's hope faded.

"OH, GOD," SAID the congressman. "This is too much."

John was sympathetic. The congressman had had to adjust his thinking so much recently.

"I think you can forget all about the Fifth Kingdom," he said comfortingly. "There are no practical implications. You certainly don't have to explain it to anyone."

"And all those birds and bugs," said the congressman despairingly. "It's somehow easier to accept that a dog or cat could ... I mean we all know that dogs can learn tricks, follow commands. ..."

"There too, it may be easier than you think," said John. "None of the animals want publicity; not Buddy or Larry either. They didn't work on the legislation to win some kind of renown."

"Imagine trying to make that credible to one of my colleagues!" exclaimed the congressman.

"Publicity never helped an animal," John went on. "They've heard about the freak shows, the laboratories ... I'm not constituted to tell lies, but I can let your colleagues assume that I'm the author of that legislative packet, and if there's something I don't understand I can ask Buddy or Larry." He looked at the congressman and smiled. "Then all you have to explain is a flying dough man."

"That doesn't seem so daunting," said the congressman. "We all grew up on superheroes. And you're so compelling in the flesh ... in the dough." His face fell again. "But the Land of the Plant People ...?"

"Take a group there," suggested John, "a congressional delegation. They can see for themselves. You don't have to vouch for the situation and neither do I. The president left behind a note saying where he was going. I can show the delegation how to get there. And, by the way, whoever goes should be heavily armed. There's nothing so unpredictable as agents 'Free from the Bonds of Reason,' as their motto goes."

The congressman was starting to feel okay again. John's calm benign presence was an antidote for almost anything.

"All right," he said. "No mushrooms. No animals. A delegation to the Land of the Plant People. I won't press charges for my kidnapping, and the ICE agents probably won't come forward now, if they didn't earlier. The whole thing is humiliating for them: not only being stranded in a tree by a man made of bun dough, but the whole situation. Do you think they want to spend their time breaking up families? That stuff's pretty hard to stomach."

THAT LEFT SEVERAL witnesses unaccounted for, one of whom appeared that very moment on the TV screen in the next room.

"That's them!" whispered Larry to Buddy. "That's Fred and Sandy!"

"Your family?" asked Buddy.

Larry nodded.

Fred explained how he and his kids had been trying to get their cat down from a tree, and the flying man had appeared and offered to help. The stranger had climbed into the tree and Fred had heard the two of them talking about politics.

"The two of *them*? The two of whom?"

"The man and our cat."

"Wait," said the reporter, who was realizing that Fred was the story here. "The cat can talk?"

"Well, I can't understand what he says. You know, he meows. But I could hear some of the other guy's side of the conversation. They were talking about Trump. I could tell that."

"Hmm," said the reporter smiling.

"The other thing is that when your cat's stuck in a tree, and someone goes to save him, you expect the person just to help the cat down … you know, physically."

"What do you mean?"

"Well, this was more psychological. Like the cat was standing on the ledge and the flying man was talking him out of it."

"Your cat wanted to kill himself?"

"No. That's not what I meant. But he didn't want to come down at first. The flying man talked to him kind of soothingly and then he wanted to come down."

"Sounds as though you have a pretty special cat."

"Well, he is really smart. He used to help my daughter with her math homework." This was a bit much for the reporter. She brought the conversation back on track.

"So why do you think the stranger wanted to kidnap your cat, if that's what happened?"

"I don't know," said Fred. "Maybe he wanted to work with him. I saw a movie once where this scientist is kidnapped and forced to develop weaponry for—"

"Unfortunately, our time's up. I'm talking to Fred and Sandy Miller, right outside of Philadelphia. Fred thinks he talked to the mysterious flying man. . . . "

"Poor Fred," said Larry. "He's a good guy. Just a little at loose ends. Weekend lawn care doesn't make up for his boring job. He's really good with the kids."

"Well, his wife loves him," said Buddy. "I was watching her face: all worried and loyal."

"I've wondered whether I could help him find a new job," said Larry, "when all this is over. Anyway, I should get home as soon as I can. They need me."

WHEN THE CONGRESSMAN came back into the living room he felt constrained with the animals. Surely he should acknowledge the role that they had played, now that he knew, but what was he supposed to do, pat them? He ended up nodding at them awkwardly from across the room with an expression on his face intended to convey respect.

31. JOHN DOUGH AT THE CAPITOL

IT WAS AS THE CONGRESSMAN HAD HOPED. SOME MEMBERS OF Congress were eager to meet the mind behind the legislation. Others were eager to find out whether they could put their names on the completed bills without being challenged or exposed. They all wanted information about the Land of the Plant People. They agreed unanimously to invite John Dough to the Capitol. Both legislative houses were operating by consensus now. It just seemed to be the most practical method. Then no one complained later about what had been decided on and everyone tried to make things work. Discussion improved too. It was quite a revelation to all of them, after so many years of acrimony and dysfunction.

They housed John in a Congressional guest room. The congressman booked a room for Alida and Buddy and Larry in a hotel near Capitol Hill that allowed pets. That way they would be on hand for John to consult. The other delegates stayed at a bird sanctuary in Maryland, where the congressman made arrangements for their feeding.

"I want to hear about everything, when you get back!" said Mary to Alida, when they said good bye.

'You will," said Alida.

WHILE CONGRESSIONAL LAWYERS worked over-time drafting bills, two senators, two representatives, and the general, made a trip to the Land of the Plant People, now named 'Trumplandia', with John and an appropriately armed security force. Based on their subsequent reports to the House and Senate, emergency funds were allocated to build a comprehensive wall around its borders. The Mexican government even made a small contribution toward its erection, as a token of friendly support for the American people, who had gone through so much recently. Construction started immediately.

The members of the congressional delegation didn't talk about their trip any more than they had to. They had seen a nation that embraced speech unfettered by the bonds of reason or truth, where pleasure, prestige, and power were the impetus behind every action and utterance, and it stuck with them like a nightmare.

Trumplandia Forever

And then she realized that she'd spend the rest of her life lying about Donald Trump to plants who neither minded that she was lying nor thought that she was clever to lie.

By God, I'd rather slave back there for another man— some dirt poor farmer who scrapes to keep alive— than to rule down here over all the witless plants!

But is the rule of any earthly potentate secure? There is always a worm in the garden. Who knows when some young Plant Person might not discover the joys of rationality? Go ahead, Plant People, if such a time comes, depose your king. Just don't send him back to us!

Psst! Hey, kid! You know rational consistency can have great power and beauty.

33. PRESS COVERAGE

"Mysterious visitor to the White House the day before Trump's disappearance has been identified by a White House official as John Dough...."

"Eye witnesses connect John Dough with intruder at Town Hall who abducted Iowa congressman...."

"John Dough seen on Capitol Hill...."

"The general confirms that former President Trump stepped down of his own accord and now lives abroad with his associates ... 'No, not Russia,' he said...."

"Flying man sighted in Philadelphia has been connected with John Dough...."

"'He smelled strongly of bun dough,' reports police officer who was present at the town hall."

"Scientists meet to discuss properties of yeast...."

"Strong man connected with Trump now appears
to be working with Congress...."

"The Republicans Cave In"

"The Democrats Cave In"

"in what seems to have been a completely
undemocratic process"

"secrecy characteristic of the Trump administration"

"lack of transparency"

"Allegedly 'full of dough'... Is he a foreign business
associate of Trump's?"

"Is this the end of our republic?"

"What the hell is going on?"

"WTF?" (That was a new online publication.)

34. THE MALL

ALIDA AND BUDDY WERE TAKING AN EARLY MORNING WALK across the Mall. It was one of those pleasant balmy mornings that forebode excessive heat in the afternoon. The park was peaceful now, but they could see that something big was going to be happening later in the day. Workmen were engaged in erecting a huge stage near the obelisk, on which technicians were preparing to set up a powerful PA system.

"What's going on?" Alida asked.

"There's going to be a huge protest. Hundreds of thousands expected," a workman told her before hurrying on again.

As they approached Capitol Hill, they saw a group of people clustered around a wooden structure in the grass. Alida and Buddy walked over to investigate. Two grownups and some kids were taking turns painting a plywood box about the size of a small SUV.

"She's not staying in the lines!" a boy was saying indignantly, while a little girl behind him painted on defiantly.

"Everyone gets a turn," said the woman, probably his mother.

"But she's messing it up!"

"I am not!" said the little girl painting a little faster and staying in the lines a little less.

"What are you making?" asked Alida, whose main peacekeeping strategy had always been distraction.

"An oven," answered the boy, and he held out a printed-out photograph of a standard electric stove. "This is what it's supposed to look like."

"What's it for?" asked Alida.

"Just a toy," interposed a man sitting on a straw bale nearby, "just a toy."

Buddy was sniffing a bucket of water.

"He can have a drink," said the man.

Buddy drank from the bucket and then he and Alida walked back to their hotel. On their way back, they passed a few people carrying signs. One said *RESCUE TRUMP*, another said *WHERE IS CONGRESS?* and a third said *DOUGH HOME!*

"I didn't like that last one," said Alida uneasily.

35. RUMOR AND PROTEST

Fury finds its weapons
—VIRGIL

THERE HAD BEEN PLENTY TO PROTEST BEFORE. THE PRESIDENT, much of his cabinet and staff, and several members of Congress had disappeared, and the official explanation was pretty far out. Congress was working in unprecedented secrecy. And somehow connected to it all was a shadowy figure, a strong man: John Dough. People said that he was housed at the Capitol, controlled Congress, was in and out of the White House. It was sinister and alarming. Some deplored him as a former confidante of Donald Trump and a friend of the notorious Iowa congressman. Others were convinced that he had kidnapped Trump, maybe even killed him—perhaps at the behest of Congress. Fantastic stories spread: he was the richest man in the world; no, he was *literally* made of dough—*bun dough*; he could fly.

And now into this dry tinder of rumor was tossed a firebrand. Congress had voted unanimously to make John Dough the next president! People gasped and exclaimed as they read the breaking news on their phones or heard it on the radio. Across the country, they poured into the streets, in concern and outrage. In Washington D.C., the crowds that were gathered on the National Mall turned their whole attention to this new menace. People who had been concerned with more abstract principles of democracy hastily revised their signs: *NO HALF-BAKED PRESIDENT!* they wrote in angry capitals, *BURN THE BUN! WE DOUGHN'T KNEAD A CEREAL KILLER IN THE WHITE HOUSE! YOU'RE TOAST!*

"Well, we're prepared, if we get a chance," said the man at the oven.

"I've been praying," said his wife.

By prior arrangement liberal and conservative speakers alternated on the huge stage.

JOHN HAD JUST finished his address to the assembled House and Senate and was still standing at the lectern, when the news was brought to the body that the protest in the Mall was swelling and taking on a dangerous cast. Evidently protesters had dismantled an extensive wooden fence, erected to protect new grass, and wielded the pickets as improvised swords. A large contingent organized by the gun lobby was there, including the new women's group, Pistols and Lipstick, who could be recognized by their large handbags.

"Let me go down and speak to them," John said to the legislators. "It's safer for me than for anyone else, since I can't be shot. I think I could reassure them." The lawmakers accepted his offer and thronged around him almost worshipfully as he stepped out onto the sill of one of the big windows in the chamber. They were sure that they would never see him again alive. It wasn't just the danger— it was that this gentle dough man was too good to be true: too wise, too sweet, too brave. They watched in silence as he flew out toward the seething mob, his patchwork cape streaming behind him.

John's plan had been to fly directly to the stage and address the crowd over the PA system, but almost immediately, he heard a cry of distress below. Somehow it reached him through all the menacing uproar of the crowd, now increased by the sight of him.

"Help! Help!" It came from below.

"Help! Help!" It was a child's voice.

John looked down and saw a sort of wooden box about the size of a car.

"Heeeelp!" It was coming from there. John swooped down.

"In there!" cried a man urgently, pointing into the dark back of the box.

John leaned in to look. Wham! Something hit him from behind, knocking him into the box. A lid swung down.

"We got him!"

"What a fool!"

John heard the sound of hammering. They were nailing the lid in place.

The boy emerged from his hiding place behind the box.

"Good job!" said his mother, excitedly. "Good job!"

John didn't know what they intended, but it was clear to him that he wouldn't have time to ooze through the seams of the box. It would take hours and they would see his dough emerging.

36. THE OVEN

THE CONGRESSMAN HADN'T WAITED WITH HIS COLLEAGUES to see John off. Instead, he had slipped out of the chamber, dashed down the hall, and made his way as fast as he could out of the building. He was determined to be near John. The congressman was pushing his way through the protesters, aiming for the stage at the other end of the Mall, when he saw John fly down into the crowd. He gasped and started to hurry toward the spot where he thought John must be.

A chant started up near the box and spread through the crowd: "BAKE THAT DOUGH MAN! BAKE THAT DOUGH MAN!" Some people repeated it as a figure of speech; others knew that it was to be taken literally. "BAKE THAT DOUGH MAN! BAKE THAT DOUGH MAN!"

THEY WERE JUST pushing the last bale of straw against the box when the congressman made his way through.

"Stand back everyone!" yelled the man who had built the box. "We're going to light this loaf on fire!"

"I just love the smell of fresh baked bread!" laughed a woman.

"FRESH BAKED BREAD! FRESH BAKED BREAD!" someone started up.

And then "BAKE THAT DOUGHMAN!" resumed. Several hundred thousand people were chanting in unison.

The congressman saw the man open a box of matches. A little boy pulled on his sleeve.

"Daddy, I wanna do it! I wanna be the one to light the dough man."

"Sweetie, it wouldn't be safe. Stand with your mother."

The congressman saw the man leaning down with the match, "Here we go...."

With a sudden burst of strength, the congressman broke through the ring of spectators and threw himself on the man with the match; they both crashed to the ground. As they struggled to their feet, the congressman swung with his fist and hit his adversary in the eye. In a second, there were five men on the assailant, holding him down.

"You wanted a front row seat? You got it!"

"BAKE THAT DOUGH MAN! BAKE THAT DOUGH MAN!" the crowd continued.

"I'm on this!" said a bald man, striding forward to take the place of his injured comrade. He yanked something from his pocket and held it out. The congressman saw that it was a lighter. He struggled again, but his guards just tightened their grip on his arms. He wasn't going anywhere.

"No!" he said. But it was almost a whisper. All the energy had left his body. He loved John as every human being loves goodness, when they really see it. And now they were going to kill him. The world would be darker. He couldn't stand it. Time slowed down. The bald man stood leering, with his legs apart and his chin jutting out, like a braggart in a bar, but, instead of drink, it was the energy of the mob that intoxicated him. He flicked the lighter and then held the little flame aloft like a torch as he approached the straw bales around the oven. He crouched down, looked back at the crowd dramatically, and then reached out with the lighter and lit the straw. A little orange flame sprang up. The bald man moved along the line of bales and crouched down again to set fire to a new spot and hasten the conflagration.

"AAAARGH!" he screamed suddenly, leaping up. He danced around, flailing his arms and yelling. What was happening? The crowd could see a swarm of insects now—stinging insects! At the same time a dark form swooped down on the lit straw—a large bird— it beat out the fire with its wings. More birds arrived. They dive-bombed the congressman's captors, who scattered in terror. *The delegates! It was the delegates!* The congressman jumped up and ran toward the oven. He had seen the hammer lying on the ground. He grabbed it and started to pry open the door.

"John!" he yelled.

"I'm still here!" John called back.

In the background there were screams and panic and the flapping of wings. Farther away in the crowd, the chanting continued, "BAKE THAT DOUGH MAN!" The congressman pried out the last nail and lifted the door. John Dough swooped out and flew toward the obelisk and the stage. The birds and insects followed him. A shot was fired at the flock but no one was hurt. The congressman started toward the obelisk on foot.

37. TIMELY ASSISTANCE

ALIDA AND BUDDY HAD COME TO THE PROTEST EARLY AND stationed themselves in a spot close to the stage. They had been standing in the heat and listening to menacing denunciations of John all afternoon and feeling helpless. There had been a moment of hope when John had appeared in the air near the Capitol, but he had disappeared almost immediately into the crowd and had not reappeared. They heard "BAKE THAT DOUGH MAN!" start up and consume the mob. Where was John? A dull dread settled in Alida's stomach. She covered her eyes with her hands and tried to think.

"If only I could talk to them! If I could just explain to them about John.... We have to try to reach the stage," she said at last.

How like Alida, Buddy thought, to place her last hope in the power of the direct appeal. But, despite his skepticism, he started to move, relieved to have a plan. The crowd was closely packed. He found that, if he wiggled through people's legs, Alida could then pull herself up to him by the leash. Their progress was very slow, but they didn't have much ground to cover. "BAKE THAT DOUGH MAN!" was all around them, beating against their ears. On top of everything else, Buddy was worried about Alida. She wasn't young, and she looked exhausted.

WITH THE UTMOST difficulty they made it around to the back of the stage, and spotted the stairs, only to encounter a new obstacle. A policeman was raising his voice over the noise of the crowd at a man in a dark suit:

"Absolutely no one is allowed on stage without a pass, no exceptions. That applies to you too! NO!" Buddy and Alida stood still. Alida drew in her breath in what was almost a sob. She felt faint. She had never learned to carry water with her like the younger generation. She tottered slightly. She needed to sit down, but that was out of the question; she would get stepped on. A very tall man, in a black Harley Davidson t-shirt, looked at her concerned.

"Hey, you okay?" he shouted over the chanting.

"Yes," she said inaudibly and smiled bravely to show that she was fine. The last thing she needed was someone calling 911 on her. He wasn't convinced.

"Look," he said. "I'm a big guy. Sit down between my feet—your dog too—and have some water." Alida hesitated. "Either that or I'm calling an ambulance," he added sternly.

Alida sat on the ground between his feet with Buddy next to her, completely safe under the A-frame of their protector's Paul-Bunyanesque legs, and he handed a big military canteen of water down to her. After she had drunk several long draughts, he took the canteen back and poured some water into his baseball cap for Buddy. "Here you go, bud," he said. After a few minutes Alida tapped his ankle and he helped her up. The stranger's assistance had been enough to keep her going, and now she had an idea. She gave Buddy instructions, and they approached the policeman.

"Excuse me, sir!" shouted Alida.

"WHAT?" shouted the policeman.

"EXCUSE ME, SIR! Do you know where we can buy water?"

"Where you can WHAT?" the policeman bent down to hear what she was saying. Alida let go of the leash and Buddy bounded up the steps. The policeman turned to look.

"My dog!" said Alida starting after him.

"You can't go up there!" shouted the policeman. "YOU—"

And then, a strange thing happened. Although the policeman had never suffered from allergies until the fall, he suddenly began to sneeze with an overwhelming violence. It was by far the worst attack he had ever had. When he recovered, the little elderly woman was gone.

After summoning the delegates, Bo Legativus had posted himself under the stairs to the stage in case he was needed. He now peered out from the dark below the metal scaffolding and waved in thanks to the leaf mold he had so effectively deployed.

When Alida reached the stage, she saw Buddy lying next to the microphone stand. He was not the kind of dog who used his good looks as a tool to accomplish his ends, but he had felt no scruples on this occasion. He lay with a feigned tranquility at the front of the stage and looked around with soulful brown eyes.

"Aww!" said the people in the crowd close enough to see him. "Aww! Look at the dog!"

"Aww!" said the black-clad technicians in charge of the PA system.

Alida walked across the stage, smiling apologetically and pointing at Buddy, as though to say, "So sorry! How embarrassing! Just getting my dog." Then she proceeded to the microphone and grabbed it from its holder.

"I am John Dough's mother!" she said, and her voice rang across the Mall. The multitude was instantly quiet. At that moment, Alida caught side of John in the air flying toward her. Behind him was the flock of delegates. A shot rang out in the distance. Buddy sprang to his feet, a dog of action once again.

"Fellow citizens . . . " Alida said, feeling a rising hope and courage, "fellow citizens, let John Dough speak to you. He's a superhero, and a good one too. This is all a misunderstanding. Give him a chance!" The crowd could see John Dough now. They started to shout again, but Alida had done some good. She was one of those older women with a beautiful voice: a little deepened with age, it had a girlish quality too. It conveyed warmth and spirit and a total lack of pretension. She was someone you could trust. And she had interrupted the momentum of their rage. She moved aside as John took her place at the microphone.

38. JOHN DOUGH SPEAKS
TO THE PEOPLE

So Neptune speaks and, quicker than his tongue,
brings quiet to the swollen waters, sets
the gathered clouds to flight, calls back the sun.
—VIRGIL

JOHN DOUGH SPOKE FAST: "I DO NOT WANT TO BE PRESIDENT! I
will not be president! I've turned them down. I just said 'no' to Congress. That's the end of it. It was a terrible idea!" The crowd was still
shouting; he wasn't sure that they had heard him. He was worried
about everyone's safety: Alida's, Buddy's, the delegates', the safety
of the whole assembled crowd. He wanted them to get the point.
Grabbing the mike from its holder, he rose slowly up into the air
and hovered six feet above the podium. The crowd became quiet.

"I want you to know," he said into the silence, "that I've turned
down the presidency—just now to Congress—officially. I will not be
president. I don't want to be. It was not a good idea."

They got the point. They turned to each other to discuss this
new state of affairs. He held up his hand to silence them.

"I'd like to say just a few words before I go home. Here we are all
together. And you," he said, indicating their placards and their weapons, indicating the big make-shift oven, "you have said quite a bit to
me. Maybe it's fair for me to say a little back."

"Let him speak!" the crowd roared. "Let him speak!" It was very important to them, of course, that he had declined the presidency—that threat had been lifted and they were proportionally disarmed. But the fact was that John Dough—with these few words and the way he said them—had already started to work his magic on them. They could tell, in whatever inexplicable way people can tell, that he was sincere and that he wanted the best for them. They felt that this dough man had more than the usual measure of light, and they wanted to hear what he had to say and to be enlightened and maybe warmed. Besides, and not insignificantly, they had never been in the presence of a real superhero before. "Let him speak!" they shouted.

John looked around at the crowd: hundreds and thousands of expectant faces. He was filled with a desire to say something that would lift them up and help them out, and his voice, when he spoke, was full of the warmth that arises from such a desire.

"IT'S BEEN VERY difficult these last months," he said, now standing behind the podium, "and you're all rightly worried about the health of your republic. I know that Donald Trump is safe and happy, having moved abroad of his own accord. And as for the members of Congress: I'm sure you could tell that they needed some kind of retreat. *(Unrest in the crowd. John Dough holds up his hand to silence them and at the same time rises about a foot off the stage, lowering himself again when they are silent.)* But I will not here insist on any version of recent events. Instead, I would like to propose a starting point for your joint work together, your work as citizens. Hear me out! *(John Dough beams warmly at the crowd, and they are quiet.)*

"There are just two ideas that are essential to this country, and we should all be able to agree on them. They are the only true basis for everything else, for all the forms of government and laws and traditions. First, the idea that all people have equal worth; and second, that everyone has a right—that can't be taken away—to life, liberty, and the pursuit of happiness. Everything else is either an attempt to work those ideas out or a failure to work them out. These principles are the first source and the final standard.

"There are many things that get in the way of our focusing on these principles.

"There are people who forget the point of our nation's laws and traditions. They are ready to forget all about the equal dignity and importance of each human being, if some smaller thing—much less self-evident- can, at its expense, be protected or procured. For instance, the right to purchase a semi-automatic with minimal inconvenience.

"Then there are people who look at our founding fathers—how they were embroiled—and how they have embroiled our nation and its laws—in genocide and slavery—and can't tolerate their names to be spoken. These people can't be inspired—or inspire their children— with the two founding principles

All people are of equal worth, and
Everyone has the right to life, liberty,
and the pursuit of happiness,

because they've gotten the idea that the principles themselves were polluted by the failures of the people who enunciated them. But it's only with the help of these principles that we can correct the harm that our forefathers did, or atone for it, or even censure it. We need these principles in order to *see* our country's "every flaw," certainly to "*mend*" them (in the words of the old song). And it is also surely true that our founding fathers deserve our lasting gratitude for their audacity and idealism in founding a country dedicated to principles so revolutionary, so lastingly potent and salubrious. They've shown us the way out of crises in the past and they'll show us the way out of this one too.

"Finally, there are people, who, for the first reason, or the second, or some other reason altogether, simply don't take these ideas very seriously, seriously enough to ask: 'What's the basis of this equality that makes every single person entitled to life, liberty, and the pursuit of happiness?' Because if there is no basis, then it's just empty rhetoric, or, an American cultural convention, like parades on the fourth of July or toasted marshmallows.

"'Fourscore and seven years ago our fathers brought forth upon this continent a new nation conceived in liberty and dedicated to the proposition that all men are created equal.' Lincoln understood that this was the point. Did he believe it? Do we? On what basis are we equal to one another? When I was very young, I learned from my family that there is an inner light in each person. When I got older, I asked myself what this light was, and I decided that the inner light must be the ability every person has to search for and respond to the truth, to recognize good and bad, and to love not just our own children and grandparents, but other people's too. Everyone has the potential for these things. No matter how bad I am, I might become good. My worth lies in this possibility. And, since every person has this potential, every person has worth of the same kind: the worth that consists in the potential to look for the truth, to choose what's right, to love.

"It's very important for us to see what the basis for this fundamental equality is, because if we see that it's this potential that every single one of us has, then we won't start thinking that there is anyone who is excluded from the right that this equality bestows: the right to life, liberty, and the pursuit of happiness. We won't start thinking that there's any sort of person who really doesn't matter, or that there is any sort of person who has forfeited his or her right. The right is inalienable because it lies in a possibility that can't be given away or destroyed.

"It's been hard for Americans to cling to this insight. Even as they wrote it down, they were killing Indians and enslaving Africans—doing the most terrible things. We do the most terrible things whenever we lose sight of the fundamental equality of all people.

All people are of equal worth and *Everyone has the right to life, liberty, and the pursuit of happiness.*

"Maybe some of you have had the experience fishing that you sometimes think you have a fish on when you don't, but that when you really do have a fish on it's absolutely obvious that you do. Or, if you're not a fisherman, consider this: you may think you're awake when you're dreaming, but that doesn't mean that you don't really know that you're awake when you are. I may be wrong—we have all been wrong—about both little things and big things, but when I contemplate the proposition that all people are of equal worth, I know that I'm awake and that I have a fish on. No skeptic can shake me from it.

"This has to be our starting point. It's a good starting point, and it's all we have. Our founding fathers gave it to us."

NOT EVERYONE IN the crowd understood what he had been saying, but they all understood where the words came from.

"I didn't get that part about the fish," said the woman at the oven, wiping her eyes, "but I love him." Her husband was clapping too hard to hear what she had said. He could stand now but he had a black eye developing from the congressman's assault.

Alida took the conspirators' list out of her pocket and checked off number three: "Unify Americans behind essential American principles." John Dough wouldn't have been so presumptuous about the success of his speech, she knew, but the crowd was wild with approbation and delight. And after his speech had been digested and promulgated by the news media, she was pretty sure it would have a lasting effect.

39. ENTERTAINMENT

BUDDY HAD READ AN ARTICLE ONLINE ABOUT THE IMPOR-tance of celebration at the end of any great labor. Evidently, in most traditional agricultural societies, at harvest time, when the people have been working hard day after day and are physically exhausted, they still dance and sing and stay up late, when the work's all done. It's a necessary step before they can rest. Buddy nudged John's leg with his muzzle. The crowd saw John Dough bend down toward the brown dog on the stage. It looked as though the dog was talking into his ear. Then the dough man came back to the microphone. He held up his hand and everyone was quiet.

"Let's have some entertainment!" John said to the crowd. "If you just stay where you are, I'll get together a flying show! Delegates, come to the stage please!"

The crowd wasn't budging. They saw a flock of birds and insects fly to the stage in response to the dough man's command, and they knew that they were in for a treat.

AFTER A LITTLE while, John Dough indicated that the show was about to begin. First, the audience heard a loon's wild and linger-ing call reverberating across the Mall from the reflecting pool. As its last undulations faded away, another sound grew in the silence: faint at first and then louder and louder, until it filled the air around them, sweet and full, with no distortion. What was it? They made out a harp, a bassoon, woodwinds . . . *antique* and *unfamiliar* woodwinds, a musicologist in the crowd noted wonderingly. Everyone recognized the tune: Yankee Doodle! Such a lively old-fashioned version! Almost immediately a line of birds appeared in the sky: hawks and kites. As they reached the obelisk, they veered and flew over the crowd; suddenly in unison they dropped straight down in a synchronized nosedive and then swooped up again, each completing a circle before proceeding on his or her way. They repeated this maneuver at regular intervals, each time eliciting gasps of delight from the spectators. As they disappeared over the Capitol dome, the music changed to a lively country dance tune. At the same time, a flock of songbirds appeared and took their place above the crowd. The crowd watched as they separated into two groups. One group flew in a circle and the other group approached them in a line. The line of birds then flew twisting around the circle of birds, as though putting a rim on a basket.

"Where's the music coming from?" Alida asked. She and John Dough were sitting in folding chairs on the edge of the stage with Buddy at their feet.

"Isn't it lovely?" John answered tactfully. Even Alida, he thought, might not be ready to learn about the spore orchestra.

Dusk was falling as the songbirds finished their performance, but the insects hadn't been idle. They had recruited all the available fireflies from Washington and the surrounding suburbs. These now appeared overhead like a ball of flickering fire. They hadn't mastered synchronized movement, but even a lopsided and uneven ring of fireflies is a magnificent and impressive sight, and the spore orchestra helped out by playing *This Little Light of Mine.* Alida went up to the microphone and invited the crowd to join in.

She called out the first line of each verse to them and then they all sang together.

This little light of Mine, I'm gonna let it shine!
This little light of mine, I'm gonna let it shine!
This little light of mine, I'm gonna let it shine!
Let it shine, let it shine, let it shine!

Hide my light in a bushel? NO! I'm gonna let it shine!
Hide my light in a bushel? NO! I'm gonna let it shine!
Hide my light in a bushel? NO! I'm gonna let it shine!
Let it shine, let it shine, let it shine!

Out there in the dark, I'm gonna let it shine!
Out there in the dark, I'm gonna let it shine!
Out there in the dark, I'm gonna let it shine!
Let it shine, let it shine, let it shine!

Hundreds and thousands of voices sang together in the Mall.

Everywhere I go, I'm gonna let it shine!
Everywhere I go, I'm gonna let it shine!
Everywhere I go, I'm gonna let it shine!
Let it shine! Let it shine! Let it shine

The people were happy and hopeful. They cried as they sang. The congressman cried in the dark at the back of the stage. Across America people were crying in front of their television sets and smart phones and computers. Larry, alone on the king size bed in front of the big TV screen in Alida's hotel room, was not crying. He stood with his tail straight up and his head in the air in a pose of exultant triumph.

The fireflies were getting more adept. Now they were flying over the crowd in a twisting ribbon of tiny blinking lights.

A technician, dressed in black, and sniffing a little with emotion, whispered to Alida that there was a screen behind her on which lyrics could be projected.

"Perhaps *America* would be appropriate," he suggested.

He projected the lyrics on the screen, and Alida led the crowd in song.

> *O beautiful for spacious skies,*
> *For amber waves of grain,*
> *For purple mountain majesties*
> *Above the fruited plain!*
> *America! America!*
> *God shed His grace on thee*
> *And crown thy good with brotherhood*
> *From sea to shining sea!*
>
> *O beautiful for pilgrim feet,*
> *Whose stern, impassioned stress*
> *A thoroughfare for freedom beat*
> *Across the wilderness!*
> *America! America!*
> *God mend thine every flaw,*
> *Confirm thy soul in self-control,*
> *Thy liberty in law!*

"I've written some new verses. Do you think I could put them up?" the technician asked. He was an aspiring poet and he saw his chance.

"Sure," said Alida.

O beautiful for principles
Laid out by dead white men.
Where they were blind, the path we'll find.
Their blunders we will mend.
America! America!
Pursue their shining path!
Past wrongs reject, but don't eject
The baby with the bath!

O beautiful for immigrants
Of every race and creed.
Don't put dumb bans on any lands,
Don't banish those in need!
America! America!
Let's cherish what we've got:
We're not a white and Christian land;
We're mixed and polyglot!

"Maybe we should end with the first verse again," said Alida to the technician.

"Sure," he said.

O beautiful for spacious skies,
For amber waves of grain,
For purple mountain majesties
Above the fruited plain!

America! America!
God shed His grace on thee
And crown thy good with brotherhood
From sea to shining sea!

The people were happy. John looked at them and felt an expansive joy. He could tell that his yeast was multiplying fast. Soon his dough would collapse. He stood up and stepped quickly to Alida's side. He leaned over and kissed her cheek.

"You are a heroine!" he said.

Then he crouched down to where Buddy lay relaxed at Alida's feet and put his big hand on the dog's back.

"And just wait until they start to feel the effects of the new legislation!"

John walked to the edge of the stage, only looking back at them for a moment, his yellow face shining with love. Then he raised his arms over his head and soared swiftly up into the air. The final expansion of his yeast gave him new power. The delegates had just arranged themselves in a heart-shaped formation fringed with glowing fireflies. Alida and Buddy saw John pass through the center of the heart before disappearing into the night sky. They stood there for a moment looking after him, and then Buddy turned and looked up at Alida questioningly.

"Dough doesn't last forever," she said, and he saw that there were tears sliding down her cheeks.

Then, as the two of them stood there without speaking, the congressman approached. He seemed to understand what had happened. He handed Alida a jar.

"Here," he said, "John gave this to me a few days ago. He asked me to give it to you when the time came."

Alida looked at the contents of the jar and unscrewed the lid. Buddy sniffed; his eyes widened and he wagged his tail.

"Sour dough starter!" said Alida.

"Yes," said the congressman. "And he said that he would leave his cape...."

But Buddy had already found it under the chair where John had been sitting. He was bringing it to Alida in his mouth.

40. PUBLIC MONUMENTS

TWO STATUES WERE ERECTED
that year, one in the Land of
the Plant People and the other
in Washington DC.

THE

END

EPILOGUE

CONGRESS'S SECOND CHOICE FOR PRESIDENT WOULD GO down in history as *The Environmental President.* His genius lay in reminding the American people how much they cared about the *beauty of the earth* and the *glory of the skies*, and in helping them to find a more satisfying and less destructive way of inhabiting them. And it turned out that there were all kinds of new jobs to be had in renewable energy. (*Who could have guessed?!*) The term *human ecology* was used to describe a concept that became important in the new era for people of every class, region, and political persuasion. They realized that it was helpful to see human beings and all their characteristic activities as part of the ecosystem of the world: it was helpful because it was accurate. It was the conceptual framework of all the new bills Congress was unrolling. It turned out that one of the by-products of recognizing the interconnectedness of things was a stunning efficiency. If you approached things from the right angle, it was possible to serve everyone's interests at once. It was exciting!

The new president announced that his first official trip would be to Paris. He wanted to convey in person the renewed commitment of the United States to the Paris Accord. He invited Alida to accompany him. She presented a tiny bit of heroic sour dough starter to President Macron, who sent it throughout France. *Brioche a l' Héros*

Just one more medal.
I'm traveling to Paris next week. I would be honored if you would accompany me.
Heavens! I don't deserve this. I'll give them to Buddy when we get home.
It's about time someone other than me recognized how great she is!

Americain was all the rage and seemed to have a good effect on everyone who ate it. No one remembered the exact moment when the last remnant of xenophobic nationalism withered in France. At some point it just came to seem silly and passé, like phrenology or powdered wigs. Buddy made a lasting friendship with a poodle named Yvette.

And if you doubt the veracity of this tale, go visit the congressman in Iowa. He loves to talk about John Dough. He's still in Congress, but now he serves his constituents much better than he did before. Any one of them will tell you that. His district, like so many others, is thriving—thanks to Alida, Buddy, and the wonderful John Dough.

NOTES

DEDICATION

"Dear Mother" by Jimmy Cliff, *Follow My Mind*, Rhino/Warner, 1975.

CHAPTER 4

within the Land of Penn. . . .
"The Pennsylvania Pilgrim" by John Greenleaf Whittier, *The Pennsylvania Pilgrim and Other Poems*, James R. Osgood, Boston, (1872).

There's a light that is shining. . . .
"The George Fox Song" by Sidney Carter, (1964).

For there was freedom. . . .
"The Pennsylvania Pilgrim" by John Greenleaf Whittier.

All men have a natural and indefeasible right. . . .
The Pennsylvania Constitution of 1776

She explained to him why the Continental Army had decided never to torture or mistreat prisoners of war.
For Washington's "Policy of Humanity," see David Hackett Fischer's *Washington's Crossing*, New York, Oxford University Press (2004), pp 275-276.

Walk in the light, whoever you may be!

John has modified the refrain of "The George Fox Song" by Sidney Carter.

CHAPTER 11

elk as big as. . . .

"A Letter from William Penn," William Penn, *The Peace of Europe, The Fruits of Solitude, and Other Writings*, edited by Edwin B. Bronner, Vermont, Everyman, (1993), p. 122.

Have you heard of the Paxton Boys?

Ben derived his information about the Paxton Boys and the relationship between William Penn and the Delaware Indians, as told in this chapter, from Kevin Kenny's *Peaceable Kingdom Lost: The Paxton Boys and the Destruction of William Penn's Holy Experiment*, New York, Oxford University Press (2009).

I know not a language. . . .

Penn, p. 123.

The Christians. . . .

Penn, p. 128.

go and smite Amalek. . . .

Cited by Kenny p. 184-185 as an example of the sort of scriptural passage the Paxton Boys' critics claimed that they would cite.

Among the charred remains. . . .

Kenny, p. 136.

Walk cheerfully over the earth. . . .
Ben paraphrases the famous statement (1656) of George Fox, the
founder of Quakerism (The Society of Friends): "walk cheerfully over
the world answering that of God in everyone...."

We know the forests north and south
"Song of the Passenger Pigeons" by Lucy Bell Sellers, 2017.

CHAPTER 16

That's Latin for 'Woolly mushroom'. . . .
I found this translation on Michael Kuo's blog *The Mushroom Expert*
at http://www.mushroomexpert.com/strobilomyces_floccopus.html
Kuo, M. "*Strobilomyces 'floccopus'*: The old man of the woods," (2013,
December).

CHAPTER 17

I looked behind him in the Woods. . . .
From "The Old Man of the Woods" by the author.

CHAPTER 19

Messengers, away and fly. . . .
Verse by Lucy Bell Sellers, 2017.

CHAPTER 20

I could not count or name. . . .
The Iliad by Homer, Book 2, 488-92, translated by A. S. Kline, Poetry in
Translation, (2009).

CHAPTER 23

A Little Bit of Monica. . . .

"Mambo No. 5" by Lou Bega, *A Little Bit of Mambo*, Lautstark, 1999.

CHAPTER 29

Wear it as long as you can. . . .

There is no evidence for the authenticity of this popular story about William Penn and George Fox. It is probably apocryphal.

Oh You Can't Hurry Love. . . .

"Oh You Can't Hurry Love" by the Supremes, *A' Go-Go*, Motown, 1966.

CHAPTER 32

By God I'd rather. . . .

The worm adapts Achilles's words to Odysseus in the Underworld in Homer's *Odyssey*, Book 11, 489-491, translated by Robert Fagles, New York: Penguin Group, (1996).

CHAPTER 38

So Neptune Speaks. . . .

Virgil, *The Aeneid*, Book 1, 142-143, translated by Allen Mandelbaum, Bantam, (1961).

CHAPTER 39

This little light of mine. . . .

"This Little Light of Mine" By Harry Dixon Loes and Avis Christiansen, c. 1920.

"America the Beautiful" words by Katharine Lee Bates, 1895.

EPILOGUE

The call it a "global integrated carbon-observing network."

Yvette had been reading Declan Butler's article, "Climate scientists flock to France's call" in *Nature: International Weekly Journal of Science,* Vol 547, Issue 7663, July 18, 2017, https://www.nature.com/news/climate-scientists-flock-to-france-s-call .

ACKNOWLEDGMENTS

MY FAMILY REALLY HELPED ME A LOT. YOU WOULDN'T BELIEVE the extent of it! A thousand thanks to: Lucy Bell Sellers, Lois Jarka, Hannes Jarka-Sellers, Peter J. Jarka-Sellers, Sophonisba M. Jarka-Sellers, Mortimer N. S. Sellers, Therese Sellers, Wanja Sellers, William Newlin Sr., Louisa Newlin, William Newlin Jr., and Therese A. Gordon. My father Peter H. Sellers will always be present in my mind, guiding, encouraging, and inspiring me. My friends also helped me a lot. Many thanks to: Sara Gordon, Bill Haines, Nathaniel Kahn, and Sid Strickland, who generously commented on my ideas and my manuscript. Just listing their names makes me feel fortunate. William Newlin Jr., who has always been kind and encouraging to his littlest cousin, was my patron. Thank you, Billy! He introduced me to the wonderful Designer Domini Dragoone. I always knew that she would make my book look as nice as it could; she was also helpful, gracious, and reassuring at every turn. Many thanks to my alert copy editor, Connie Thompson. *Gratias vobis omnibus maximas!*

ABOUT THE AUTHOR

LUCY BELL W. JARKA-SELLERS
has lived most of her life in the
Germantown section of Philadelphia. She now lives in "Upper
Germantown" (AKA Mount Airy)
with her family and their animals.

CPSIA information can be obtained
at www.ICGtesting.com
Printed in the USA
BVHW03s1313151018
530226BV00001B/73/P